EMILY PRAGER'S

A VISIT FROM THE FOOTBINDER

"What we have here then in Emily Prager's collection is the collaboration of an ideologue, a comedian and a literary artist...Splendid and original."

— THE NEW YORK TIMES

"Prager is a thoroughly contemporary Aristophanes—a subtle voice of comic satire serving delight and horror from the same vibrato....And style, always, always elegantly in service of the story itself. It's 'Lysistrata' with a vital updating: This time the satirist is a woman....This stands with the best of Swift and Lamb."

— LOS ANGELES TIMES

"Prager has an original and energetic vision....She has got that rare combination of style *and* substance....These fantasies are wickedly funny. They are wonderful."

— LOS ANGELES HERALD-EXAMINER

A VISIT FROM THE FOOTBINDER

and other stories

Emily Prager

Vintage Contemporaries

VINTAGE BOOKS · A DIVISION OF RANDOM HOUSE
· NEW YORK

For Mom and Dad
and, especially, for Tom

First Vintage Contemporaries Edition, October 1987

Library of Congress Cataloging-in Publication Data
Prager, Emily.
  A visit from the footbinder, and other stories.
  (Vintage contemporaries)
  Originally published: New York : Simon and Schuster, 1982.
  I. Title.
PS3566.R25V5 1987 813'.54 87-40110
ISBN 0-394-75592-8 (pbk.)

The author and publisher wish to express grateful acknowledgment for
permission to quote from the sources listed below:

The *I Ching* or *Book of Changes*, the Richard Wilhelm translation into English
by Cary F. Baynes. Bollingen Series 19. Copyright 1950, © 1967 by Princeton
University Press, © renewed 1977 by Princeton University Press.

Lysistrata by Aristophanes, translated by Dudley Fitts. Copyright © 1962 by
Harvest Books, Harcourt Brace and World. Copyright © 1954, 1955, 1957,
1959 by Harcourt Brace and World.

Author photo copyright © 1985 by Ralph DePas

Manufactured in the United States of America
10 9 8 7 6 5 4 3 2 1

Acknowledgments

My deepest thanks for their constant support, hard work, unflagging good humor and high standards to my editor, Larry Freundlich, and his assistant, Sheila Nealon; to my agents Jay Acton and Asher Jason; to my friends Anne Beatts, Tom Davis, Winkie Donovan, Victoria Prewitt, Nora Elcar, Carol Caldwell, Michael O'Donoghue, Teri Keani, and Dr. Bill Evans; for a stunning cover to Frank Morris; and for allowing me poetic license to Jerzy Kosinski and Russell Baker.

Contents

O blessed Zeus, roll womankind
Up into one great ball;
Blast them aloft on a high wind,
And once there, let them fall.
Down, down they'll come, the pretty dears,
And split themselves on our thick spears.

—Chorus
Lysistrata
(Aristophanes; translated by
Dudley Fitts, 1962)

A Visit from the Footbinder

"I shall have the finest burial tomb in China if it's the last thing I do," Lady Guo Guo muttered triumphantly to herself. It was midafternoon at the height of the summer, and the Pavilion of Coolness was dark and still. She tottered over to the scrolls of snow scenes which lined the walls and meditated on them for a moment to relieve herself from the heat.

"Sixteen summers in the making, sixteen memorable summers and finally ready for decor. Oh, how I've waited for this moment. I think blue for the burial chamber overall, or should it be green? Ah, Pleasure Mouse, do you think blue for Mummy's burial chamber or green?"

Pleasure Mouse, aged six, second and youngest daughter of Lady Guo Guo, pondered this as she danced a series of jigs around her mother. "Blue would be lovely on you, Mummy, especially in death. Green, a bit sad and unflattering, I think."

"You are so right, Pleasure Mouse. Green reeks of decay. Such an unerring sense of taste in one so young—I see a fabulous marriage in your future. In two or three seasons, after Tiger Mouse has been wed," Lady Guo Guo looked away. "Revered Mummy," Pleasure Mouse was leaping up and down and tugging at her mother's very long sleeves, "At what hour will the footbinder come tomorrow? How long does it take? Can I wear the little shoes right away? Will I be all grown up then like Tiger Mouse?"

Lady Guo Guo shuffled quickly toward the teakwood table

on which lay the blueprints of the pavilions erected to date. Pleasure Mouse ran in front of her and darted and pounced at her playfully like a performing mongoose at his colleague the performing snake.

As a result of this frolicking, Lady Guo Guo lost her balance and, grabbing on to the edge of the table to steady herself, she snapped angrily, "No answers, Pleasure Mouse! Because of your immodest behavior I will give no answers to your indelicate questions. Go now. I am very displeased."

"Yes, Mummy. I am sorry, Mummy," said Pleasure Mouse, much chastened, and, after a solemn but ladylike bow, she fled from the Pavilion of Coolness.

Pleasure Mouse raced across the white-hot courtyard, past the evaporating Felicitous Rebirth Fishpond, and into the Red Dust Pavilion, which contained the apartments of her thirteen-year-old sister, Tiger Mouse. Inside, all was light or shadow. There were no shades of gray. The pungent aroma of jasmine sachet hung on the hot, dry air like an insecure woman on the arm of her lover. As usual, Tiger Mouse was kneeling on the gaily tiled floor, dozens of open lacquer boxes spread around her, counting her shoes.

As Pleasure Mouse burst into the chamber, Tiger Mouse glanced up at her and said haughtily, "I have one thousand pairs of tiny satin shoes. If you don't believe me, you can count them for yourself. Go ahead," she said with a sweeping gesture, "count them. Go on!" Wavering slightly, hair ornaments askew, she got to her feet. Then she went on: "I have the tiniest feet in the prefecture, no longer than newborn kittens. Look. Look!"

Tiger Mouse toddled intently to a corner of the chamber in which stood the charcoal brazier used for heating in winter. Now, of course, it lay unused, iron-cold in the stifling heat. For a moment, she encircled it with her arms and rested her cheek and breast against the cool metal. Then she reached beneath it and amid a chorus of protesting squeaks brought out two newborn kittens, one in each hand, which she then placed beside each of her pointy little feet.

"Come," she cried. "Look," and she raised her skirt. Pleasure Mouse ran and squatted down before her. It was true. The newborn kittens, eyes glued shut, ears pasted to the sides of their heads, swam helplessly on the tiled floor, peeping piteously for milk. They were far more lively than Tiger Mouse's feet but certainly no bigger. Pleasure Mouse was terribly impressed.

"It is true what you say, Older Sister, and wonderful. No bigger than newborn kittens—"

"No *longer* than newborn kittens," Tiger Mouse barked.

"Indeed," Pleasure Mouse responded in a conciliatory tone and then, by way of a jest to lighten the moment, added, "Take care the mother cat does not retrieve your feet." Pleasure Mouse laughed sweetly and ran trippingly alongside Tiger Mouse as the latter, smiling faintly, wavered back to her many shoes and knelt before them.

"Tiger Mouse," Pleasure Mouse twirled around in embarrassment as she spoke, unsure of the consequences her questions might elicit, "The footbinder comes tomorrow to bind my feet. Will it hurt? What will they look like afterwards? Please tell me."

"Toads."

"What?"

"My feet are like the perfect Golden Lotus. But yours, horned toads. Big, fat ones."

"Oh, Tiger Mouse—"

"And it didn't hurt me in the least. It only hurts if you're a liar and a cheat or a sorcerer. Unworthy. Spoiled. Discourteous. And don't think that you can try on my shoes after, because you can't. They are mine. All one thousand pairs."

"Yes, Tiger Mouse." Pleasure Mouse dashed behind her and snatched up one pair of the tiny shoes and concealed them in the long sleeve of her tunic. "I must go for my music lesson

now, Older Sister," she said as she hurried toward the chamber
door. She stopped just short of exiting and turned and bowed.
"Please excuse me."

"But perhaps," said Tiger Mouse, ignoring her request, "the
pain is so great that one's sentiments are smashed like egg
shells. Perhaps for many seasons, one cries out for death and
cries unheeded, pines for it and yearns for it. Why should I tell
you what no one told me?"

"Because I'd tell you?" answered Pleasure Mouse. But Tiger
Mouse went back to counting her shoes. The audience was
over.

Pleasure Mouse scampered out of the Red Dust Pavilion,
past the evaporating Felicitous Rebirth Fishpond, and through
the gate into the recently completed Perfect Afterlife Garden.
When she reached the Bridge of Piquant Memory, she stopped
to catch her breath and watch as her mother's maids watered
the ubiquitous jasmine with the liquid of fermented fish in
hopes that this might make it last the summer. The stench was
overpowering, threatening to sicken, and Pleasure Mouse sped
away along the Stream of No Regrets, through the Heavenly
Thicket and into the Meadow of One Hundred Orchids, where
her friends, the One Hundred Orchid Painters, sat capturing
the glory of the blossom for all time.

Aged Fen Wen, the master painter, looked up from his
silken scroll and smiled. For sixteen years, he had labored
on Lady Guo Guo's burial tomb, at first in charge of screens
and calligraphic scrolls, and now, since they were done, of wall
hangings, paintings, window mats, and ivory sculpture. He
had watched as Pleasure Mouse grew from a single brush-
stroke to an intricate design, and though he was but an artisan,
he considered himself an uncle to her.

For her part, Pleasure Mouse adored Fen Wen. No matter
where the old man was at work on the great estate, no matter
how many leagues away, as soon as she awoke in the morning
she would run and find him. During the winter when her
family returned to the city, she missed him terribly, for al-

though she loved her father, she rarely saw him. With Fen Wen there was no need to observe formalities.

Fen Wen was sitting, as was each of the ninety-nine other Orchid Painters, on an intricately carved three-legged stool before an ebony table on which lay a scroll and brushes. There were one hundred such tables, and in front of each grew a single tree, each one supporting an orchid vine, each vine bearing one perfect blossom. The trees grew in twenty rows of five across, and aged Fen Wen was giving leaf corrections at the southwestern corner of the meadow, where Pleasure Mouse now found him and, without further ado, leapt into his lap.

"Venerable Fen Wen," she said as she snuggled into his chest and looked deep into his eyes, "guess what."

Fen Wen wrinkled his Buddha-like brow and thought. "The emperor has opened an acting school in his pear garden?" he said finally.

"No."

"You have fallen in love with an imitator of animal noises?"

"No, no," Pleasure Mouse giggled happily.

"I give up," said Fen Wen, and Pleasure Mouse wiggled out of his lap and skipped in place as she related her news.

"The footbinder is coming tomorrow to bind my feet. And afterwards I shall wear tiny shoes just like these," she produced the pair she had stolen from Tiger Mouse, waved them before Fen Wen, then concealed them again, "and I will be all grown up—"

Pleasure Mouse halted abruptly. Fen Wen's great droopy eyes had filled with tears, and the Orchid Painters around him modestly looked away.

"Ah," he sighed softly. "Then we won't see you anymore."

"No. What do you mean? Why do you say that?" Pleasure Mouse grabbed on to Fen Wen's tunic and searched deeply into his eyes.

"At first, of course, you will not be able to walk at all, and then later when you have healed, you may make it as far as the front Moon Gate, but, alas, Pleasure Mouse, no farther. Never as far as this Meadow. Never as far. They won't want you to. Once your—"

"Won't be able to walk?" said Pleasure Mouse quizzically. "What do you mean? Lady Guo Guo walks. Tiger Mouse walks . . ."

Now began a silence as aged Fen Wen and the ninety-nine other Orchid Painters turned glumly toward the east, leaving Pleasure Mouse, age six, second and youngest daughter of Lady Guo Guo, alone and possessed of her first conceptual thought. Past experience joined with present and decocted future. Nuggets of comprehension, like grains of rice in a high wind, swirled behind her eyes, knocked together and blew apart. Only this softly spoken phrase was heard on earth.

"They cannot run," she said, "but I can." And she ran, through the Meadow of One Hundred Orchids, down the Path of Granted Wishes, and out the Sun Gate into the surrounding countryside.

Just outside the market town of Catchow, a mile or so down the Dragon Way near the vast estate of the prefect Lord Guo Guo, lay situated the prosperous Five Enjoyments Teahouse. On this spot one afternoon in the tenth century, three hundred years before the teahouse was built and our story began, a Taoist priest and a Buddhist nun were strolling together and came upon a beggar. Filthy and poor, he lay by the side of the road and called out to them, "Come over here. I am dying. I have only this legacy to leave." The beggar was waving something and the Taoist priest and the Buddhist nun moved closer to see what it was.

"Look," said the beggar, "it is a piece of the very silk with which the emperor bade a dancing girl swaddle her feet that they might look like points of the moon sickle. She then danced in the center of a six-foot lotus fashioned out of gold and decorated with jewels." The beggar fell backward, exhausted by his tale, and gasped for breath. The Taoist priest and the Buddhist nun examined the dirty, bloody, ragged scrap of cloth and glanced at each other with great skepticism. "Ah yes. It is an interesting way to step from Existence into Nonexistence, is it not?" said the Buddhist nun. "Indeed," replied the Taoist priest. "So much easier to escape Desire and sidle closer to Immortality when one can follow only a very few paths. But alas, in time, this too will pass."

There was a rattle in the beggar's throat then, and his eyes rolled upward and grasping the scrap of silk, he died.

The Taoist priest and the Buddhist nun murmured some words of prayer over the beggar's body, linked arms and continued their travels. The ragged scrap of bloody cloth fluttered to the ground and was transformed by the Goddess of Resignation into a precious stone that lay at that very spot until the year 1266, when it was discovered and made into a ring by the famous courtesan Honey Tongue, star attraction of The Five Enjoyments Tea House, which had been built nearby some years before.

Pleasure Mouse, taking extreme care not to be seen, scrambled up the back stairs of The Five Enjoyments Tea House and sneaked into the luxurious apartments of her father's good friend, the famous courtesan, Honey Tongue. She startled the beauteous lady as she sat before her mirror tinting her nails with pink balsam leaves crushed in alum. "Oh!" exclaimed Honey Tongue. "Why, it's Pleasure Mouse, isn't it? Sit down, little one, you're out of breath. What brings you here?"

Pleasure Mouse collapsed on a brocade cushion and burst into tears. The beauteous lady floated to her side and hugged her warmly to her perfumed breast. "Oh dear," crooned Honey Tongue, rocking back and forth, "oh dear oh dear oh dear," until finally Pleasure Mouse was able to speak: "Tomorrow, the footbinder comes to bind my feet and—"

Honey Tongue brought her hands to her mouth and laughed

behind them. She rose from Pleasure Mouse's cushion and, still laughing, wafted back to her seat before her mirror. She fiddled for a moment with her hair ornaments and began to apply the stark white Buddha adornment to her face and afterward the deep-rose blush.

As all this seemed to contain great meaning, Pleasure Mouse ceased speaking and ran to her side, watching in the mirror everything the lovely lady did. When she was done plucking her eyebrows and smoothing on the final drop of hair oil, she smiled the loveliest of sunny smiles and said, "It's a bargain, Pleasure Mouse. The pain goes away after two years, and then you have a weapon you never dreamed of. Now, run along home before someone sees you here."

Pleasure Mouse did as she was told, but as she was speeding along the Dragon Way, trying to reach the eastern Sun Gate of the estate before she was seen, she had the bad fortune to run smack into the sedan chair procession of her father's older sister, Lao Bing. Her old auntie had come all the way from the city for the footbinding, and when she peered out the window of her sedan chair and saw Pleasure Mouse, she bellowed in an imperious tone, "Halt!"

The bearers halted abruptly and set the sedan chair down in the middle of the Dragon Way. An enormous donkey cart, that of the night-soil collector, which had been following a few lengths behind the procession, now was forced to halt also, and a vicious verbal battle ensued between the chair bearers and the night-soil collector and his men as to who had the right of way. Lao Bing paid no attention to this melee. She opened the door of the sedan chair and cried out, "All right, Pleasure Mouse, I see you. Come over here this minute."

Pleasure Mouse ran to the sedan chair and scampered inside. As she closed the door, Lao Bing bellowed, "Drive on!" and the bearers stopped quarreling with the collector, hoisted the sedan chair poles onto their knobby-muscled shoulders, and continued in a silent run to the estate.

The sedan chair rocked like a rowboat on a storm-tossed sea. Pleasure Mouse began to feel queasy inside the dark box. The odor of Lao Bing's hair oil permeated the heavy brocades, and the atmosphere was cloying. The old one's hair ornaments jiggled in emphasis as she spoke.

"Really, Pleasure Mouse, young maidens of good family are not allowed outdoors much less outside the estate grounds. Oh, if your father knew I had found you on the Dragon Way . . ."

"Dearest Auntie," entreated Pleasure Mouse, "please don't tell. I only thought since the footbinder is coming tomorrow and I'll no longer be able to—"

"Footbinder?" Lao Bing seemed perturbed. "What footbinder? You don't mean to tell me your mother has *hired* a footbinder for tomorrow?" Pleasure Mouse nodded.

"Really, that woman spends like a spoiled concubine!" Lao Bing peeked through the curtain on the window and sighed in resignation. "All right, Pleasure Mouse, we are inside the Sun Gate now. You may get down. Halt!" The bearers halted and Lao Bing opened the door.

"Auntie?" Pleasure Mouse hesitated before the door. "What is it like?"

Lao Bing mulled the question over for a moment and then replied briskly, "It is something a woman must endure in order to make a good marriage. No more. No less, Pleasure Mouse. If you wish to live at court, you must have tiny feet. Logic, indubitable logic."

"And does it hurt, Lao Bing?" Pleasure Mouse gazed stoically into her aunt's eyes and prepared herself for the reply. The old lady never minced words.

"Beauty is the stillbirth of suffering, every woman knows that. Now scamper away, little mouse, and dream your girlish dreams, for tomorrow you will learn some secret things that will make you feel old."

Lao Bing closed the door of the sedan chair and gave the

order: "Drive on!" Pleasure Mouse circled the Meadow of One Hundred Orchids, traversed The Heavenly Thicket, and made her way to the recently constructed Avenue of Lifelong Misconceptions, where she passed the afternoon contemplating her future footsize.

Lady Guo Guo was receiving in her burial chamber. It was bleak in the dense stone edifice, dim, musty and airless, but it was cool and the flaming torches affixed to the walls gave off a flickering, dangerous light. A party of silk weavers from Shantung milled nervously in one corner while their agent haggled with Lady Guo Guo over a quantity of mouse-vein-blue silk. In another corner, the head caterer waited to discuss the banquet of the dead and dodged attempts by a group of nosy flower arrangers to guess the menu. There were poetry chanters, trainers of performing insects, literary men—throngs of humanity of every occupation crammed into the burial chamber and its anteroom, hoping to be hired for a day's labor. And many had been. And many were. One local glue maker had quite literally made his fortune off Lady Guo Guo in the last sixteen years. He had retired early, well fed and happy. And he was but one among many.

It was through this teeming mass of gilders, cutlers, jugglers, sack makers, pork butchers and pawnshop owners, that Lao Bing now made her way preceded by three servants who, rather noisily and brutishly, made a path. Lady Guo Guo, distracted by the commotion, looked up from her bargaining, recognized her sister-in-law, and hurried to greet her.

"Welcome, venerable, husband's sister, to my recently completed burial chamber. Majestic, is it not? I shall enter the afterlife like a princess wearing a gown of," Lady Guo Guo snapped the bolt of silk and it unrolled like a snake across the cold stone floor, "this blue silk. My color, I think you'll admit. Thank goodness you have come with all your years of wisdom behind you," Lao Bing sniffed audibly, "for I need your advice, Lao Bing. Do we do the wall hangings in the blue with a border in a green of new apples or a green of old lizards who have recently sluffed their skin? Question two: Who shall do my death mask and who my ancestor portrait? Should the same man do both?"

"Old lizards and different men," said Lao Bing decisively, and tottered over to a sandalwood stool and sat on it. "Little Sister," she began, a note of warning in her voice, "these days the lord, your husband, reminds me of a thunderclap in clothes. Day and night the creditors camp outside the door of the prefecture. He asks why you do not use the rents from the rooming houses you inherited from your father to pay these merchants?"

"What? And deplete my family's coffers? The lord, my husband, is as tight with cash as the strings on a courtesan's purse, Lao Bing, and no tighter. Do not deceive yourself."

"Well, really," said Lao Bing, her sensibilities offended, and her message delivered, abruptly changed the subject. "They say that the fallow deer sold in the market is actually donkey flesh. It's a dreadful scandal. The city is buzzing with it. And as if that weren't enough—" Lao Bing lowered her voice, rose from her seat, and ushered Lady Guo Guo away from the throngs and down into the depression in the vast stone floor where her coffin would eventually lie. "As if that weren't enough," Lao Bing continued, sotto voce, "the emperor is using his concubines to hunt rabbits."

Lady Guo Guo was horror-struck. "What? Instead of dogs?"

Lao Bing nodded solemnly.

"But they cannot run."

"Ah, well, that's the amusement in it, don't you see? They cannot possibly keep up with the horses. They stumble and fall—"

Lady Guo Guo swayed from side to side. "No more please. I feel faint."

"You are too delicate, younger brother's wife."

"For this world but not for the next." Lady Guo Guo patted the lip of the depression to emphasize her point.

"Hmm, yes," said Lao Bing, "if it is up to you. All of which brings me to the subject of tomorrow's footbinding. Pleasure Mouse tells me you've *hired* a footbinder."

"Really, Lao Bing, expense is no object where my daughter's feet—"

"I have no concern with the expense, Little Sister. It is simply that the Guo Guo women have been binding their daughters' feet themselves for centuries. To pay an outsider to perform such an intimate, such a traditional, such an honorable and serious act is an outrage, a travesty, a shirking of responsibility, unlucky, too arrogant and a dreadful loss of face."

"Lao Bing." Lady Guo Guo climbed out of the depression with the help of a sack maker who hurried over to ingratiate himself. "You are like an old donkey on the Dragon Way, unable to forge a new path, stubbornly treading the muddy ruts of the previous donkey and cart. This footbinder is a specialist, an artist, renowned throughout the district. And what is most important in this mortal world, I'm sure you'll agree, is not who does or does not do the binding, but the size of Pleasure Mouse's feet once it's done."

Lao Bing clapped her hands, and her servants appeared by her side, hoisted her out of the depression and set her down once again on the cold stone floor. Her hair ornaments spun with the impact. "Very well," she said after some moments of icy reflection. "But let us hope that with your modern ways you have not offended any household spirits."

A breeze of fear gusted across Lady Guo Guo's features. "I am not a fool, Lao Bing," she said quietly. "In the last few days I have burned enough incense to propitiate the entire netherworld. I have begged the blessing of ancestors so long departed they failed to recognize our family name and had to be reminded. The geomancer claimed he had never seen anything like it—before he collapsed from exhaustion."

"And he is sure about tomorrow?" Lao Bing asked, and then regretted it.

"Really, Lao Bing." Lady Guo Guo turned on a tiny heel and scurried back to her bargaining table. With a snap of her fingers, she summoned two maids and instructed them to show Lao Bing to her apartments in the Red Dust Pavilion. The old lady, suddenly fatigued by her journey, waddled slowly over to her sister-in-law's side and said gently, "Forgive me, Little Sister. It is a festival fraught with sentiments, worse this time perhaps because it is my perky Pleasure Mouse."

But Lady Guo Guo had returned to her business. "I'll take the green of old lizards," she was saying to the silk weavers' agent, "at three cash per yard and not a penny more." Haggling began anew and echoed off the great stone walls. Lao Bing departed, preceded by her servants, who elbowed her way into the crowd, which parted for a moment to admit her and then closed behind her again. Just like, thought Lady Guo Guo, a python who swallows whole its prey.

In the hot, dry center of the oven-baked night, Pleasure Mouse tossed and turned and glowed with tiny drops of baby sweat. Ordinarily, the nightly strumming of the zither players out in the courtyard would have long since lulled her to sleep, but not this night. She was far too excited.

She sat up on her lacquered bed, crossed her legs, and removed from beneath her pillow, the tiny pair of shoes she had stolen from her sister. She stroked them for a moment, deep red satin with sky-blue birds and lime-green buds embroidered over all, and then placed them on the coverlet in the strongest of rays of blue moonlight.

"How sweet," she murmured to herself, "how beauteous. Soon I will embroider some for myself and I will choose . . . cats and owls. So tiny, I do not see how—"

And she glanced around to make sure she was alone and unseen, and stealthily picked up one shoe and tried to slip it on her foot. But it would not fit, in any way whatsoever. Most of her toes, her heel and half of her foot spilled over the sides. She was very disappointed. "Perhaps my feet are already too big," she sighed aloud, and might have tried once more like panicked birds who fly into the window mat and though they've gained no exit, fly again, but just then the jagged sound of breaking glass shattered her reverie, and up she sprang and hid the tiny shoes beneath her pillow.

"Who goes there?" she cried, and ran to the door of her chamber.

"Oh, great heavens, Pleasure Mouse, it's I," came the whispered reply, and Pleasure Mouse sighed with relief and slipped into the corridor. There, crisscrossed by moonlight, on her knees before a broken vial, her father's concubine, Warm Milk, age nineteen and great with child for lo these six long moons, looked up at her and wept. "Oh, Pleasure Mouse," she managed through her tears, "I've ruined the decoction. I'll never get more dog flies now in time, or earthworms, for that matter. It took weeks to collect the ingredients and I've dropped them. It's my legs. They're swollen like dead horses in the mud. And as for my feet, well, they're no longer of this earth, Pleasure Mouse," Warm Milk rolled off her knees and sat squarely on the floor, her eyes tightly shut and soft moans of agony escaping her lips as she stretched her legs out in front of her. Pleasure Mouse stared at her opulent stomach, which looked like a giant peach protruding through Warm Milk's bedclothes and wondered what creature was inside. Warm Milk bent over and began to massage her legs. Her tiny white-bandaged feet stuck out beyond the hem of her nightgown like standards of surrender at a miniature battle. "They cannot bear the weight of two, Pleasure Mouse, but never say I said so. Promise?"

Pleasure Mouse nodded solemnly. "Promise," she replied, and examined Warm Milk's feet out of the corner of her eyes.

"They stink, Pleasure Mouse, that's the worst of it, like a

pork butcher's hands at the end of a market day. It frightens me, Pleasure Mouse, but never say I said so. Promise?"

Pleasure Mouse nodded furiously. She would have liked to speak but when she tried, no voice was forthcoming. Her little girl's body had begun to contract with a terrible heat and in the pit of her stomach, feelings cavorted like the boxers she had heard of at the pleasure grounds.

Warm Milk leaned back on her hands and was silent for a moment. Her waist-length blue-black hair fell about her swollen little body and gleamed in the moonlight. Her flat, round face was blue-white, as pale and ghostlike as pure white jade. So too her hands.

"I was going to the shrine of the Moon Goddess to beg her for a boy. The decoction," she sat up and gestured at the oozy pink puddle that was beginning to travel along the corridor floor, "was to drink during the supplication. They say it always works, a male child is assured. Perhaps—" Warm Milk cupped her hands in the pink slime and brought it to her lips.

"No," cried Pleasure Mouse, horrified at such intimacy with dirt. "Please don't. You will be sick. Tomorrow I will run and find you many spiders and new dog flies too!" Warm Milk smiled gratefully at the little girl. "Will you, Pleasure Mouse?" she asked. And Pleasure Mouse remembered.

"Oh, no, I can't," she cried, blushing deeply. Her slanted eyes welled up with tears like tiny diamonds in the blue moonlight. "Tomorrow, the footbinder comes to bind my feet and—"

"You shan't be running anywhere." Warm Milk sighed resignedly and sucked the liquid from the palms of her hands. "What bad fortune, Pleasure Mouse, for us both, as it turns out. For us both. But never say I said so."

"Where are your toes?" Pleasure Mouse asked suddenly and without advance thought. It was just that she had glanced at Warm Milk's feet and finally realized what was different about them.

"My what?" asked Warm Milk nervously.

"Your toes." Pleasure Mouse squatted down before the bandaged feet and pointed a tiny finger at them. "I have five toes. You have one. Did they cut the others off?" Her eyes were wide with terror.

"No." Warm Milk pulled her nightgown over her feet. "No, of course not."

"Well, what happened to them?" Pleasure Mouse looked directly into Warm Milk's kind black eyes and awaited an answer.

Warm Milk dropped her head and basked for a moment in the blue moonlight. Out in the courtyard, the zither players were at their height, their instruments warm and responsive, their male hearts carried away by the loveliness of the tune. At length, Warm Milk spoke.

"When I was but five seasons old, the elegance of my carriage and the delicacy of my stature were already known far and wide. And so my mother, on the counsel of my father, bound my feet, which was an unusual occurrence for a maid of my then lowly peasant status. I could not run. I could not play. The other girls made mockery of my condition. But when I was ten, your father spied my little shrew-nosed feet and bought me from my father for his honorable concubine. Beneath your venerable father's wing I have nestled healthfully and prosperously for many seasons but never so happily as when I see, from the heights of my sedan chair, my big-footed playmates now turned flower-drum girls hawking their wanton wares by the river's edge."

Warm Milk laughed modestly. "Do you understand me, Pleasure Mouse?" Pleasure Mouse nodded, but she wasn't sure. "Yes, Honorable Concubine, but about your toes, where—" She began again but was interrupted by the appearance of six horrified maids who should have been on duty throughout the pavilion but who, because of the closeness of the evening, had ventured into the courtyard to watch the zither players, and had quite forgotten their charges in the romance of the moon-light and song.

The corridor rang with noises of reproach and then, like ants with a cake crumb, four of the maids quickly lifted up the concubine Warm Milk and bore her away to her apartments. The remaining two hurried Pleasure Mouse into her chamber and into her bed.

"I want my dolly," said Pleasure Mouse mournfully, and the maid brought it to her. The big rag doll, fashioned for her by aged Fen Wen, with the lovely hand-painted face of the Moon Goddess, black hair of spun silk, and masterfully embroidered robes, came to her anxious mistress with open arms. Pleasure Mouse hugged her close and sniffed deeply at her silken hair. Then she slid her hand under the pillow, pulled out the tiny shoes and slipped them on the dolly's rag feet. After a bit of stuffing and pushing, the shoes fitted perfectly. And Spring Rain, for that was the dolly's name, looked so ladylike and harmonious of spirit in the tiny shoes, that Pleasure Mouse forgot her fears and soon was sound asleep.

The footbinder was late. Already it was two hours past cock-crow, and the courtyard outside the Temple of Two Thousand Ancestors was buzzing with anticipation and excitement. The man with the performing fish had arrived early and so was understandably perturbed about the wait. So too the tellers of obscene stories and the kite flyer. Had it been another season, they might have chatted away the time, but it was mid-summer and as the hours dragged by, the day grew hotter and the energy for physical performance ebbed slowly away. The zither players were doing their best to keep up spirits, strumming at first soothingly and then rousingly in celebration of the occasion. Hands holding fans wafted back and forth in tempo to the music, pausing only to pluck cloying hair and clothing from damp and heated skin.

Inside the dark, hot temple, Lady Guo Guo stamped her

tiny foot. The din from the courtyard resounded through the walls, and she was dreadfully embarrassed before her ancestors. The geomancer, a thin, effeminate young man, shook his head and wrists.

"The propitious hour is upon us, Lady. After it passes, I cannot be responsible for the consequences."

Lao Bing, suffering mightily from the heat and certainly tired of waiting, concurred, "Really, Little Sister, we must get on with it. This is exactly what happens when you pay an outsider—oh!" Lao Bing, frustrated beyond words, ceased speaking and fanned herself wildly.

Before the altar, Pleasure Mouse sat on a stool with her feet soaking in a broth of monkey bones. She stared up at the portraits of her most recently departed ancestors, solemn in the yellow light of the prayer candles. Occasionally, her eyes traveled about the walls of the great chamber and met those of hundreds of other ancestors whom she had never known in life and of whom she had never heard.

Just after cockcrow, she had entered the temple and with the female members of her family, she had prayed to the Little-Footed Miss for the plumpest and softest and finest of Lotus Hooks. You could, Lao Bing informed her, end up with either Long Hairpins, Buddha's Heads or Red Cocoons. It all depended on the expertise of the binding, the favor of the ancestral and household spirits, and the propitiousness of the hour at which the feet were bound. The broth of monkey bones was to soften her feet, to make them malleable enough to fit into the tiny pair of red satin boots that her mother had made for her and which now sat upon the altar like an offering to the gods.

"I have paid for a footbinder, and I shall have one!" snarled Lady Guo Guo, and followed by her maids, she lurched angrily from the temple.

The sunlight caught her unawares. It struck her like the projectile of a crossbow, and she was momentarily blinded and confused. She and her small procession immediately snapped open their fans, shielded their eyes from above and held this pose, unmoving, like an operatic tableau. Those in the courtyard pushed forward and back, chattering among themselves, eagerly awaiting instructions. The zither players struck up Lady Guo Guo's favorite tune, and as her eyes adjusted to the light, she dimly perceived members of the crowd being shoved to and fro and finally propelled to one side to permit the entrance of, she focused her eyes sharply to make sure, her husband and master, the prefect, Lord Guo Guo.

Lady Guo Guo bowed as did the entire crowd and said, "Welcome, my lord, an unexpected pleasure. I had no idea you were in the neighborhood. You are stopping at The Five Enjoyments Tea House, I presume?"

"Ah, if only I could afford to," he replied pointedly. "But alas, I'm just passing through on a visit to the sub-prefect."

"Let us climb the belvedere," began Lady Guo Guo nervously, "for there we can speak in private." She hurried toward the turret, which was hard by the temple. "I call it Hereafter-View, for its beauty is quite suffocating." Lord Guo Guo followed and then stopped, carefully examining the stones at the belvedere's base.

"What stone is this?" he asked. His copyist followed, taking notes.

"Marble," Lady Guo Guo answered nonchalantly as if he ought to know.

"From?"

"From . . ." Lady Guo Guo concentrated intently. "From, from, from—forgive me, husband, I have forgotten the name. I am overwrought. Your arrival has coincided with Pleasure Mouse's footbinding. The propitious hour is upon us; I cannot—"

"Perhaps I can help you remember. It is a Chinese name?"

"No," snapped the Lady, and fled into the belvedere and up the winding marble steps. The Lord followed.

"No? Not a Chinese name, then presumably not from China. Imported then. Let me think. Annam? Champa?"

Lady Guo Guo disappeared beyond the next turn in the stairs. The Lord stayed behind.

"What?" he cried out. "Not even from the East? How luxurious! From the West, then. Ah, I know! Egypt!" Lord Guo Guo removed a knife from his sash and proceeded to carve a message into the marble wall. The knife scraped unpleasantly against the stone, and curious as to the noise, Lady Guo Guo reappeared around the bend. The message read: "Paid for by the prefect, Lord Guo Guo," and the date, "1260." The Lady gasped. "How dare you deface my belvedere?" she demanded.

"How dare you use my wealth to make the merchants rich? Pretty soon there will be no aristocracy left. At the rate you are spending, I shall be the first to go." Lord Guo Guo put away his knife.

"If you are so fearful, why do you not impose excessive taxes or put a ceiling on prices as you did last year when you bought yourself your title? As it is, I must purchase everything from the shops you own under a fraudulent name, and shoddy merchandise it is too! This marble was my one extravagance—"

"No more credit," Lord Guo Guo said simply, and Lady Guo Guo sank to her knees and sobbed.

"You men are so cruel," she cried, her tears dropping to the marble step. "Building this tomb is my one last pleasure, and you will take it from me just as you took from me my ability to walk. Well, let me tell you, you may cripple me in this endeavor, but you will never stop me."

"Men took from you your ability to walk?" the Lord said incredulously. "Is it the man who pulls the binding cloth to cripple a daughter's feet? No man could do a thing like that. No man could bear it."

"No man would marry a natural-footed woman. There is more to binding feet than just the binding!"

"If all women were natural-footed, a man would have no

choice," Lord Guo Guo concluded and began descending the stairs.

Lady Guo Guo shook with fury and called after him. "Shall I leave your daughter natural-footed then? Yes. Yes. You are quite right and logical. Let our family be the one to begin the new fashion, and we shall begin it with the perky Pleasure Mouse!" In her anger, the Lady called out theatrically to her maid, "Wild Mint! Tell the footbinder to go away; we shall not need her."

"The footbinder?" asked Lord Guo Guo quietly. "Then you will not do the binding yourself?"

"Shall the prefect Lord Guo Guo's daughter be natural-footed? Your choice, my lord."

"So." The Lord grinned. "You've hired another to do the job for you? An interesting twist."

"Natural feet or lotus hooks? Be quick, my husband, the propitious hour is passing and will not come again for a full twelve seasons of growth."

Lord Guo Guo grew impatient at this last and turned his back. "These are women's things, your affairs, wife, not mine," he muttered sullenly.

Lady Guo Guo tapped her tiny foot. "What if I were to fall ill, creating a disturbance, right this moment and allow the propitious hour to pass?"

"I wouldn't let you," Lord Guo Guo snarled.

"You could not prevent me. It is a women's ritual, my husband, and as such, depends on the good omen. A mother's falling ill during a ceremony at which no man can show his face, even a father, especially a father—"

"Would you harm your daughter to harm me? What is it you seek, wife?"

"Unlimited credit, sir. Decide quickly; there is little time left."

Lord Guo Guo's nostrils flared. "You have it, ma'am" were the words that he spat out as, robes flying, he hurtled through the belvedere door. Lady Guo Guo smiled to herself and followed quickly behind.

"Here, wife." The Lord spoke through gritted teeth and thrust a walking stick into the Lady's arms. "An ebony cane. Also imported like your marble from Africa. For the Pleasure Mouse, for after."

"Thank you, my lord," said Lady Guo Guo, bowing low, "and a good journey, sir. Please come again." And with that she was off, hobbling swiftly toward the temple courtyard before Wild Mint could send the footbinder away.

Pleasure Mouse looked around nervously at Lao Bing and the geomancer, who were whispering together.

"Well," sniffed Lao Bing, "if it comes to it, I'll do it myself then. I bound three daughters of my own with perfect success. Autumn Surprise won the Emperor's commendation for the most beauteous hooks at the Hu Street small foot contest. Now she's his concubine-in-waiting, if you don't mind."

"Exquisite," said the geomancer in his whiny voice. "But did you hear about the Sung sisters?"

"What?"

"Rivals for the same young man, Black Mist cut up all of Blue Jade's tiny shoes and heaped them in the courtyard for all to see!"

"No!"

"Yes. And speaking of concubines-in-waiting, I hear the Emperor often keeps them waiting for years, and in the harems with only each other for company, I hear they use each other's hooks for—"

"The footbinder has arrived," announced Lady Guo Guo as she entered the chamber. "Let us begin."

Lao Bing sent the geomancer a parting glance of daggers. "Leave us," she hissed and then turned to inspect the famous footbinder.

"Forgive me, everyone," the footbinder waved heartily at

those assembled as she strode into the temple. "The youngest daughter of the Wang family persists in unbinding on the sly. Each time she does this I tell her I shall only have to pull the bindings tighter. After all, we have two reputations to think of, hers and mine. But you can't tell a child about Lotus Boats, as you all know. They never believe it can happen to them."

Lao Bing, Lady Guo Guo, and the various maidservants in the chamber nodded in understanding.

"Children think we are born with small feet," began Lao Bing.

"Oh, if only we were," sighed Lady Guo Guo, interrupting.

Lao Bing continued. "But once in Shensi Province, I saw a natural-footed peasant girl, well, you talk of Lotus Boats, but really Fox Paws would be more accurate. Feet as large as a catapult repairman's."

Pleasure Mouse twisted around and stared at the footbinder. Barely four feet high and as round as a carved ivory ball, the tiny woman removed her pointy-hooded homespun cloak and revealed herself to be a Buddhist nun. Shaved head and eyebrows, saffron robes, face unadorned by powder or blush, the little fat turnip of a woman bent down and picked up her basket and hurried toward the altar.

Lao Bing gasped in horror and took Lady Guo Guo roughly to one side. "What is the meaning of this? She's not wearing shoes! She's barefooted and natural-footed. I've never been so embarrassed, and what about Pleasure Mouse? I—"

"Shh!" Lady Guo Guo took Lao Bing's hands and tried to explain. "Not having bound feet herself, she is better able to make a really good job of binding others. It is an esthetic act to her, objective, don't you see? For us it is so much more, so clouded. Our sympathy overcomes our good judgment. Pleasure Mouse's feet will be as hummingbirds, you'll see."

"All right," sniffed Lao Bing. "I suppose it makes some sense. But my aunt did my bindings, and merciless she was." Lao

Bing's voice had risen as she remembered. "I have always felt that had it been my own mama, some sympathy might have been shown for my agony."

"Perhaps," called the footbinder from across the room. "Perhaps not."

"At any rate," Lao Bing, outraged at the interruption, went on, "I blame such newfangled notions on the barbarians from the North, the Mongol hordes. I pray such contaminate influences do not sully my perky Pleasure Mouse. But if they do, I personally—"

"Silence, please," boomed the footbinder. And then, "Send away the throngs outside the temple!"

"No kiteflyer?" asked Lady Guo Guo timidly. "But we have always had a kiteflyer for before. It is the last time—"

"No. No. The feet swell from the running and it is far too difficult. As for the teller of obscene stories, he was present when I bound the Wang girls and, sadly, he is simply neither obscene nor funny."

"He seemed amply disgusting to me," mused Lady Guo Guo as she padded toward the chamber door.

"Yes, foul," agreed Lao Bing.

"Wild Mint." Lady Guo Guo's number one maidservant rushed forward and curtsied. "Clear the courtyard."

"But the man with the performing fish?"

"Keep him on retainer. Perhaps for the inaugural ceremonies."

Wild Mint nodded and rushed out. Some angry murmurs rose and fell, but soon there was bright, hot quiet outside, disturbed now and then only by the buzz of insects. Wild Mint re-entered the chamber and took up her post behind a red-lacquered pillar.

"Where is Tiger Mouse?" Lao Bing was whispering to Lady Guo Guo.

"I am afraid she is still too delicate to attend the ritual. She cannot as yet see the humor in it." Lady Guo Guo placed her finger across her lips to command silence then and turned her attention to what the footbinder was doing.

"What are you doing?" Pleasure Mouse was asking.

The footbinder trained her beady eyes on the child and answered directly, "I am tying you to the chair with leather thongs." She finished securing the last arm and leg and paused to examine her handiwork.

"Why?" asked Pleasure Mouse, pulling a bit against the bonds.

"It hurts, Pleasure Mouse, and if you writhe all over the place you will interfere with perfection of the binding. Now here, grasp these water chestnuts in each hand and when it hurts, squeeze them with all your might and if you are lucky, your feet will turn out no bigger than they are."

Pleasure Mouse took the water chestnuts and squeezed them in her palms. The footbinder scurried around in front of the altar, head bent to her task and mumbling to herself.

"Here's a handkerchief to wipe the tears. Here's my knife. The binding cloth. Alum. Red jasmine powder. All right. I think we are all ready. Is it the propitious hour?" The footbinder glanced at Lady Guo Guo, who nodded and came forward to one side of Pleasure Mouse's chair. She patted the little girl on the shoulder and smiled weakly. Lao Bing came forward as well and stood on the opposite side. "If we begin just at the propitious hour, it won't hurt," the old lady said without much conviction.

Warm Milk entered at this moment by the side door of the temple and sat without comment next to Lao Bing on a stool carried in her maidservants. Warm Milk did not look well, so swollen was she with womanly waters pressurized by the heat. But she smiled at Pleasure Mouse and waved one of her long, long sleeves.

The footbinder took up the knife and knelt down in front of the chair and concentrated on the broth of monkey bones and Pleasure Mouse's feet. She draped a towel over her knees and picked up one foot and dried it. She then took the knife and brought it toward Pleasure Mouse's toes. The little girl shrieked with terror and fought against her bonds. Her mother and her aunt held her down and tried to placate her. Warm Milk stood up hurriedly and cried out,

"Do not be afraid, Pleasure Mouse. She means only to cut your toenails. Truly, little one, truly."

Pleasure Mouse relaxed and tears ran down her face and onto the new silk robe that her mother had embroidered just for this occasion. The footbinder grabbed Pleasure Mouse's handkerchief, dabbed her cheeks and proceeded to cut her toenails.

"Now, what are the rules that all ladies must obey? Let me hear them while I cut."

Pleasure Mouse recited in a clear, sad voice:

"Do not walk with toes pointed upwards.
Do not stand with heels in midair.
Do not move skirt when sitting.
Do not move feet when lying down.
Do not remove the binding for there is
nothing esthetic beneath it."

"And because, once bound, a foot does not feel well unbound. Excellent, Pleasure Mouse," said the footbinder setting down her knife and rubbing the child's feet with alum. "I can see that once your hooks are formed, you will be quite a little temptress." The footbinder winked lewdly at Lao Bing and Lady Guo Guo. "I predict buttocks like giant pitted plums, thighs like sacks of uncombed wool, a vagina with more folds than a go-between's message, and a nature as subdued as a eunuch's desire."

The women in the temple tittered modestly, and Pleasure Mouse blushed and squirmed beneath the bonds.

Suddenly, Pleasure Mouse became mesmerized by a beaute-

ous ring on the right index finger of the footbinder's dimpled
hand. It flashed in the light of the prayer candles, and as the
footbinder laid out the silk binding cloths, it created, in midair,
a miniature fireworks display.

"What a splendid ring," murmured Pleasure Mouse.

"What ring, dear?" asked Lady Guo Guo.

"That one, there—" Pleasure Mouse indicated the footbinder's right hand with a bob of her head, but the ring had
gone, vanished.

"Never mind," said Pleasure Mouse, and squeezed the chestnuts in her tiny hands.

The footbinder took hold of the child's right foot and, leaving the big toe free, bent the other toes beneath the foot and
bound them down with the long, silk cloth. The women gathered around the chair and watched the process intently. She
then took a second cloth and bound, as tightly as she could,
around the heel of the foot and down, again over and around
the now bent toes, with the result that the heel and the toes
were brought as close together as they could go, and the arch
of the foot was forced upward in the knowledge that eventually it would break, restructure itself and foreshorten the foot.
The last binding was applied beneath the big toe and around
the heel, pushing the appendage up and inward like the point
of a moon sickle. When the right foot was done, the footbinder
bound the left foot in the same manner, removed the basin of
monkey bone broth and retrieved the tiny shoes from the altar.
She knelt before the Pleasure Mouse and, as she forced her
bound feet into the shoes, Lady Guo Guo intoned a prayer:
"Oh, venerable ancestors, smile favorably upon my perky Pleasure Mouse, that she may marry well and one day see her own
daughter's entry into womanhood. Take the first step, my
child. Take the first step."

Lady Guo Guo, Lao Bing and the footbinder untied the
leather thongs and released Pleasure Mouse's arms and legs.
Pleasure Mouse was silent and rigid in the chair.

"Up, dear," said Lao Bing, taking the child's elbow. "Up, you must walk."

"Take the first step," said Lady Guo Guo, grasping the other elbow.

"Up, child," said the footbinder, and she stood Pleasure Mouse on her newly fashioned feet.

Pleasure Mouse screamed. She looked down at the tiny shoes on her now strangely shaped feet and she screamed again. She jerked toward her mother and screamed a third time and tried to throw herself to the ground. The women held her up. "Walk," they chanted all together, "you must walk or you will sicken. The pain goes away in time."

"In about two years' time," crooned the courtesan, Honey Tongue. She had suddenly appeared in place of the footbinder who seemed to have vanished.

"Walk, little one, no matter how painful," Lao Bing grabbed the flailing child and shook her by the shoulders. "We have all been through it, can't you see that? You must trust us. Now walk!"

The women stepped back, and Pleasure Mouse hobbled two or three steps. Waves of agony as sharp as stiletto blades traversed the six-year-old's legs and thighs, her spine and head. She bent over like an aged crone and staggered around, not fully comprehending why she was being forced to crush her own toes with her own body weight.

Pleasure Mouse lunged toward the apparition and fell on the altar, sobbing and coughing. Honey Tongue enveloped her in a warm and perfumed aura.

"Do you wish to stay on earth, or do you wish to come with me?" Honey Tongue waved her long, long sleeve, and for a moment all was still. The women froze in their positions. Time was suspended in the temple.

"You can be a constellation, a profusion of stars in the summer sky, a High Lama in the great mountains to the East—a man, but holy. Or an orchid in the Perfect Afterlife Garden. Or you may stay as you are. It is your choice, Pleasure Mouse."

The little girl thought for a long while and then answered, "The only way to escape one's destiny is to enjoy it. I will stay here."

Honey Tongue vanished, and in her place reappeared the small, fat cabbage of a footbinder. The women wept and chattered, Pleasure Mouse moaned and bellowed in agony, and Time, its feet unbound, bounded on.

"Come, Pleasure Mouse. Sit," said the footbinder, and with her strong, muscled arms, she lifted the little girl and set her in the chair before the altar. The child sighed with relief and hung her head. The tiny shoes were stained with blood, as were her dreams of ladyhood. She whimpered softly. Warm Milk lurched painfully to her side, bent down and began to massage Pleasure Mouse's small burning legs. The women gathered around the altar, and the footbinder lit two prayer strips and recited:

"Oh, Little Footed Miss, Goddess of our female fate, keep the Pleasure Mouse healthy and safe. Let her hooks be as round, white dumplings. Let them not turn to dead, brown shreds at the end of her legs. Let her blood not be poisoned or her spirit. Let her learn to walk daintily without pain, and let her not envy those who can run for they are lowly and abused. Ay, let her never forget: for them, running is not luxury but necessity. Let her marry a relative of the Emperor, if not the Emperor himself. And let her have many sons that, when the season comes, she might enter the afterlife like a princess."

Lady Guo Guo snapped her fingers. "Wild Mint, escort our new lady back to her chambers, if you please. I will come later, Pleasure Mouse, when the sun goes down, and I will bring with me an ebony cane sent by your father from the city. Look, little one, here is Spring Rain. Wild Mint sent for her that she might see you in your ladylike mantle."

"My word," gasped Lao Bing, "the doll wears the tiny shoes!" Lady Guo Guo laughed. "So she does. How odd. Perhaps Tiger Mouse—"

Pleasure Mouse grabbed Spring Rain and ripped the shoes off her feet. She clasped the rag doll to her chest and stumbled from the temple.

Lady Guo Guo took the footbinder aside and paid her. The women wandered aimlessly from the temple into the sunlight.

"Oh dear," sighed Lao Bing. "I hurt all over again. As if fifty years ago were yesterday." She shielded her eyes from the sun with her fan.

"Must it always be so violent?" murmured Warm Milk.

"I don't know if it must be, but it always is," said the footbinder as she and Lady Guo Guo emerged from the temple.

"Have many young girls . . . died?" asked Lady Guo Guo.

"Some prefer death, Lady Gee, it is the way of the world." The footbinder climbed into her sedan chair. "I must be off," she said. "Keep the child on her hooks. I shall return in one week to wash and rebind. Please have the next smallest pair of shoes ready for my return. Goodbye."

Warm Milk curtsied to Lao Bing and Lady Guo Guo and with the aid of her maids, tottered past the departing procession toward her apartments.

Lao Bing and Lady Guo Guo watched the footbinder's sedan chair disappear through the Sun Gate, and when it was gone, Lao Bing clucked and said, "A footbinder. A footbinder. Ah, the seasons do change. I feel old, Little Sister. My toes are flattened out like cat tongues. The soles of my feet rise and fall like mountain peaks. How much did you pay her?"

"Thirty cash."

"Thirty cash!"

"It was worth it not to be the cause of pain," Lady Guo Guo said simply.

"Ah, yes, I see," sighed Lao Bing. "Well then, perhaps she won't blame you although—"

"After Tiger Mouse, I could not bear—you understand?"

"Of course." Lao Bing patted her brother's wife on the shoulder and, with a nod of her head, summoned her sedan chair.

"Farewell, Little Sister. We shall meet again in the city. I shall regale the Lord, your husband, with tales of the magnificence of your burial tomb, but be frugal, child, his patience falters."

"Thank you for your counsel, Lao Bing. It is well taken."

Lady Guo Guo closed the door of the sedan chair and waited until the pole bearers hoisted up the old lady and trotted away down the temple path.

The sun was iron-hot and glaring. Lady Guo Guo swept into a shadow of the temple eaves and stood there by herself, staring into nothingness, occasionally and absentmindedly waving her fan. After a time she ventured out into the sunlight, determined to make her way to the Pavilion of Coolness, where, she had decided, today she would take her rest. She padded past the Hereafter-View belvedere, across the Courtyard of a Thousand Fools, and right in front of the Zither Players' Wing, where the zither players caught sight of her and at once struck up her favorite tune. "China Nights" was the name of the song, and she waited politely in the white-hot sunlight until the final pings had died away. After bowing in thanks, she continued on, slower now, as she was losing strength. By the time she reached the Pavilion of Coolness, her hooks were puffy and throbbing like beating hearts.

The Alumnae Bulletin

Edda Millicent Mallory (Brearley, Class of '65) opened her Ethiopian basket, removed from it two ounces of the finest California-grown *Cannabis indica,* and, with the aid of her favorite Bambú papers, began to roll it into joints.

"Jesus, Faye," she said without looking up, "I haven't seen you since . . . Christmas Eve . . . five months."

"I know it." Faye O'Jones (Brearley, Class of '65) poured herself a tumbler of Glenfiddich Scotch, neat, and from a small can which she took from her purse added to it a pinch of nutmeg. "I never leave the East Sixties. You never go above Fourteenth Street. And we're both too cheap to pay for cabs."

"Also, we hate going home alone at night, especially at our age. It's déclassé."

"Definitely," said Faye and sipped her drink. "You've gotten better at that," she added.

"Yes, sadly," said Eddie and ran her tongue along the edge of the rolling paper. "It was one of my last holdouts against women's liberation. I don't open wine bottles. I don't fill ice-cube trays. I don't make salad dressing. And I think men should roll the joints—which is a problem if you want to smoke when there are no men around. I've had to learn to do it, Faye. The tenor of the times."

"With me it's filling lighters, hailing cabs, and zippers up the back. I guess I'm a romantic." Faye checked her watch. "Seven forty-five. What time is Bunny coming?"

"Between seven-thirty and eight, any time now. She had to stop at the bank to pick up her phallus. It's funny, isn't it? She keeps hers in the vault at the Bank of New York. She's there now with a bunch of Park Avenue matrons who are picking up their jewels. I'd like to see that scene."

"Good place for it. Mine lives in the freezer, at the back. I live in fear my cleaning woman will find it, my mother, or one of my nephews."

"I, of course, as a chronicler of sexual aberrations have ample excuse, but I hide mine away with my shoes. Did I ever tell you my first word was 'shoe'?"

"No. But I'm not surprised."

Edda finished rolling the last of six joints, placed them on the coffee table, and stood up. "There. That's done," she said and then added, "I think we'll want some acid, don't you, Faye? Since it's our tenth anniversary? How good's your report?"

"The best yet. You won't be disappointed. Where'd you get the acid?"

"The engineer from Rutgers who runs the Buddhist shop. You remember?"

"Ah yes, the young man with the loincloth who's into Kundalini Yoga."

"Precisely. It's quite fresh, he promised, and pure."

"Good. Then let's have it." Eddie went into the kitchen to get the acid out of the icebox. "Eddie," called Faye, "do you still . . . ?"

"No, no. He would only come see me when alternate-side-of-the-street parking was suspended. So he'd be assured of a parking place. I found that somewhat arbitrary, even mundane. So, in spite of his more esoteric abilities, I had to give him up. He wasn't Mr. Right, Faye."

Edda returned to the living room carrying a small Visine bottle, which she set down by the joints. Faye nodded. "I understand," she said and then gave a little jump. "Oh, I almost forgot. Two things." She rummaged through her purse and withdrew a tiny white envelope and a newspaper clipping, both of which she handed to Eddie. "Here's the coke. From my dealer at Grey Advertising. Best in the city. Money-back guarantee. And, as you can see . . ."

" 'Rock Star Impersonator Jailed,' " Eddie read aloud from the clipping. "Oh, Faye. You were right about him."

"Yes. But where did he get all those costumes?"

"We'll never know. Do you think you were in any danger?"

"Only when he reminisced about Vietnam. He got a bit intense. It was a little dicey. Otherwise he was very gentle."

"You met him on a horse in Central Park?"

"Umhumm."

"How odd," said Eddie and set the envelope of cocaine down next to the acid. "Is your report . . ."

"Oh, no, Eddie. Far more interesting than that, far more. A dream come true, Eddie."

"Mine too," said Eddie, checking the coffee table to make sure everything was organized. "Only a bit different than usual. Quite different, when you come down to it. Do I have everything, Faye? Help me."

"Well, let's see," said Faye and looked slowly around the room. "You have the uniforms, you have the candles, tape recorder, tapes. You have your phallus, I have mine. Bunny's bringing hers. Where's the Alumnae Bulletin?"

"Oh, that's it. I knew . . .", Eddie scurried into the bedroom and returned with a small stack of Brearley Alumnae Bulletins, stenciled paper pamphlets held together by staples and no bigger than the average Latin primer. "You know there've been six of these since we last met," she said as she piled them neatly on the table. "Have you read any?"

"One or two," said Faye and poured herself another Scotch. "It's hard not to."

"I know. The temptation is—I read one. It said I had moved to London, Faye. That I was living there happily and working."

"Really?"

"Yes. Isn't that wonderful? I don't know why, except one night, about three years ago when Neville was in town, we went to the theater and ran into Lucy Latham and her too-noticeably-Harvard-grad husband Willie, and I introduced them. The next thing I knew, the Bulletin reported I had moved to London. She naturally assumed . . ."

"It was Neville's proprietary air."

"Huumm, yes.

Beware of the Etonians,
They're awfully, awfully nice.
But underneath their stylish clothes,
Their hearts are made of ice.

And yet, and yet, once, Faye, once, when I was staying with him in London, he left early one morning on a pretext. I went for a walk and saw him on the King's Road with another woman. When he phoned that afternoon, I told him I had seen him and that I thought he was a lying little cheat. We hung up and I ran a bath and got into the bathtub. Twenty-five minutes later, the bathroom door opened and there he was. He gave me a kiss, apologized, and left. Yes, he left the office, drove all the way home to give me a kiss, which he gave me, and then drove all the way back. Total time door to door: one hour for one kiss. I was impressed, Faye. Especially since he belonged to the other woman and I was the interloper. I shall never forget it."

"Manners, Eddie, manners. English boys smell like leather and old books. They snuggle like cats on a frosty morning. Their skin is as thick and soft as clotted cream. I told you about Billy, didn't I?"

"The Rock guitarist?"

"Yes. His mother had a sheepdog. Once a week, she would go around the flat and collect all the fur it shed. Then she would have it spun into wool, with which she was knitting a blanket. He's in jail now for robbery, I think."

"Oh, Faye, you do love those criminal musicians."

"I do seem to, don't I," said Faye softly and sprinkled her Scotch with nutmeg.

"Do you have the sheet music?" asked Eddie as the downstairs buzzer rang.

"Damn. No. But I do have a pitch pipe and if we can't do it *a cappella* from memory by now, what good are we?"

Eddie pushed the talk button of the intercom. "Bunny?" she called.

"Bunny," was the reply.

Eddie pressed the buzzer and waited. "I wonder if Bunny's changed." She glanced nervously at Faye. "It's been three years."

"Sure," said Faye and lit a Du Maurier. "Haven't we? But it'll all be the same when we put on the phalluses."

The doorbell rang and Edda threw open the door. "Bunny!" she squealed. "Bunny!" And then more quietly and in a tone of astonishment, "Bunny, you look gorgeous. Your eyes—what have you done to your eyes? They're like Giancarlo Giannini's."

Bonita Warburton (Brearley, Class of '65) stood on the doorsill of Eddie's apartment, out of breath. Her thick blond hair was cropped close to her head, her skin was as tan as whole-wheat toast, and her baby-blue eyes were all iris. She was wearing a camel's-hair coat with big, padded 1940s shoulders, brown spike heels, and in her arms she carried her old bookbag, an eggplant-colored sack with a white "B" on it for Brearley.

My eyes are the proof of my report, Eddie. You'll see. God, there must be a million charity balls going on tonight. Every dowager in town was at the bank. It took hours. And then getting a cab—New York City. I'm never ready for it. The cab driver was darling—a boat person, I think. He had no idea how to get here. I had to do a running monologue. We're going to meet for cocktails tomorrow, that's his day off. Six-thirty at Arirang House—it's still there on Fifty-sixth Street, I hope?"

Eddie nodded. "Come in, Bunny," she said, and Bunny trotted through the door.

"Thank God. Ginseng cocktails are just the thing for this man, I know it. It was his Mongoloid eyes that got to me. Have you ever had an Asian, Eddie?"

"No."

"You, Faye?"

"No."

"Me neither. Think they do it sideways? Gee, I've missed you both." Bunny threw off her coat and laid her bookbag gently next to the two others that were already on the sofa. She stared at the coffee table for a moment, and then dipped her hand into the bookbag and withdrew a small brown Italian leather clutch purse. "I brought something special," she said, opening it. "One for each of us."

"Oh, Bunny," Faye exclaimed, as the little black ball was dropped into her palm, "you shouldn't have."

"Opium!" cried Eddie. "How divine!"

"Part of my divorce settlement, chicks. Arto had this cabinet full of the stuff. When I left the villa that fateful morning, I thought of you and simply couldn't resist."

"Well, perhaps we'll do it instead of the acid, or in addition to, we'll see later. I think I have pipes, but God knows where. What would you like, Bunny?" Eddie collected the three black balls and lined them up next to the cocaine packet on the coffee table.

"Wine and a joint please, Eddie. I must calm down. It's been a harrowing year." Bunny picked up a joint, lit it, and inhaled deeply. Eddie handed a corkscrew and a bottle of 1967 Chateau Rothschild to Faye. "An arrogant, if lewd, foreign wine. You be sommelier, Faye. What was it like being married to an Italian and living in Italy, Bunny?"

"Like being mentally kneecapped, Eddie. Like being held prisoner in an Italian leather boutique. I took to wearing caftans day and night. And little gold sandals with thongs between the toes. I became obsessed with hair-care products and my facial sauna broke from overuse."

"And Arto?" asked Faye, pouring the wine. "What of Arto?"

"A woman can tire of being adored, Faye. Can you understand that? My blond pubic hair seemed to surpass the Miracle of Fatima in existential importance. I thought of dyeing it, of electrolysis, of wax treatments, but I was too lethargic. In the end I ran, like a scared blond bunny, wearing the caftan and the sandals, carrying an Italian leather bag, the opium, and a recent copy of the Brearley curriculum changes which I had just received in the mail. I hopped the ferry from Brindisi and the rest is in my report. What's new with you?"

Bunny sipped her wine and passed the joint to Eddie, who took it and sat down in an armchair next to Faye. Faye O'Jones slowly crossed her long, slim legs, and toyed with her one pierced feather earring.

"Well, let's see," she said. "About a year and a half ago, we finished the Tyrannosaurus Rex. It was a great event. During a cocktail party held in the construction hall beneath the skeleton, I saw the man that I am going to marry."

"Faye, you didn't tell . . ."

"No, Eddie, this is the first time I've . . ."

"Saw the man, Faye? Just saw?" Bunny, intrigued, sat forward on the couch and took the joint from Eddie.

"Yes. Like Mrs. Sir Richard Burton who, seven years before she ever met him, spied the great explorer on a London street and knew that they would wed, so I . . ."

"Sir Richard Burton who explored Mecca and Medina? Who translated *The Arabian Nights?*"

"Yes. He would leave London and telegraph her, his wife. 'Pay. Pack. And Follow,' was the message. And she would. But seven years before they ever met, she saw him on a street and knew."

"And this man, your man?" Eddie grabbed the joint from Bunny.

"Smoked a pipe and gave me hope. He stood by himself, his tall, lanky frame bent over, examining intently the final bone in the Rex's tail. For a long time I stared at him, unable to breathe, or speak, my limbs suddenly paralyzed by a heretofore unknown emotion. Tears ran down my cheeks, clouding my view, and when I wiped them away and looked up again, he was gone. A year and a half has passed since then. Now we are on the twenty-fifth vertebrae of a brontosaurus ordered by a museum in Minneapolis. I spend all day on a ladder contemplating a time when giant lizards roamed the earth. It's lonely and alienating work, but somebody's got to do it. Edda?"

"Congratulations, Faye," began Eddie nervously, "on your engagement. Bunny, you've been married. Have you any advice to give, any cautions?"

"Just remember: *Post coitum, omnis feminam est triste.* It's hormonal, not the end of the world."

"That's rather depressive, isn't it, Bunny?"

"Well, Eddie, I'm just divorcing now. I'm not in a period of high euphoria. Or perhaps I am. It's hard to tell anymore. And you, Eddie, what's new with you?"

"I am in the middle of my eighteenth novel. This one is a departure from the rest in that it takes place in a dressing cubicle at Vidal Sassoon. This, the result of a trip Mrs. Bainbridge made to America last fall. It's reminiscent of Beckett, don't you think?"

"How is Mrs. Bainbridge?" asked Bunny.

"Mrs. Bainbridge is in hog heaven, Bunny. She's an international star. Beloved as the writer of the Finchley pornoromance series, she has dyed her hair red and just managed to squeeze a swimming pool in the driveway of her council house. She's doing all the right things, and the press adores her for her love of fame. She's just wonderful on the talk shows. I saw her in London—she enjoyed it so much in a way I never could. I'd want to teach them, you see. She wants to tell them stories. It's quite different."

"How much do you pay her to be you?" asked Bunny.

"Fifteen percent of the gross: a tidy sum. We're translated into ten languages these days. The Americans like us least. But the Spanish and the Italians keep us in hair dye and then some."

"Eddie," asked Faye, "why on earth don't you want to take credit for the Finchley porno-romance series? Aren't you proud of it? I'm proud of my dinosaurs."

"Of course I am," Edda replied. "But Mrs. Bainbridge is prouder, and more energetic and more devoted. She was a charwoman for twenty-five years before she became me. She appreciates it so. She has humility. And she looks so lovely in designer clothes, like the richest of Third World wives. Her round little body bulges out in all the wrong places. She gives Dior a homey look, and often touches the cloth of the clothes surreptitiously as if to make sure she's actually wearing them. I love her. I often wish I was her. But if I was, I wouldn't be able to write the books. I suppose that's the irony of it."

"Schizophrenia at its most productive—ingenious," said Bunny. "Can I have the joint now, Eddie? You've been Lauren Bacalling it for an hour."

"Oh. Is that the feminine of . . ."

"Yes. Are you in love, Eddie?"

"No, Bunny. I wouldn't have set up the meeting if I were. Our reports are less mushy if we're not, I think. A hard edge coming from a pure, clean mind . . ."

"Like Nazi campfire girls?" asked Faye, taking the joint from Bunny.

"Very like Nazi campfire girls when you come right down to it. I have noticed over time that when this group falls in love, they're not good for one damn thing. Pushovers and slugs. Bruised fruit."

"I agree with Eddie," said Faye. "Love turns my character to eels. Always has. Suddenly, I can't return a phone call, can't keep a date, and I certainly couldn't give an honest report. No,

I couldn't be in love, Bunny, and attend a meeting. I'd be afraid the man would find out and feel betrayed, or worse that I'd betray you two by being reticent."

"What—with all these drugs—reticent?" Bunny glanced at the coffee table.

"Calm down, Bunny, you're among friends now. Chop this up. You'll feel better." Eddie took a single-edged razor blade from her Ethiopian basket and handed it to Bunny. From her Brearley bookbag, Bunny removed a heart-shaped mirror and set it, glass up, on the coffee table. Deftly, she poured the cocaine out of the packet and created a tiny white hill on the surface of the mirror. She began to chop.

"Bunny," asked Edda, "did you do any carving this year?"

"Oh yes," said Bunny as she divided the cocaine into lines. "The first few months I did some tortured madonnas for the villa. Really nice traditional ones. Out of olive wood. I would carve only at night because I didn't want anyone watching me—didn't want comments or any other interest. I spent more and more time alone. And pretty soon, I began to lead the life of a tortured madonna carving a tortured madonna—as if I had to experience the condition before recreating it. As if I didn't trust my imagination to make its own logic. I became dangerous to myself, Eddie. I had to stop. Here, it's ready." She passed the mirror to Faye, who sniffed a few lines and passed it on to Eddie, who did the same and gave it back to Bunny. "Do you think it's possible to be too sensitive to be an artist?" asked Bunny.

"I think it's time to begin," said Eddie. "Let's take a little acid and get changed." The others nodded. Faye finished her Scotch, Bunny her wine, and Eddie took the Visine bottle and squeezed out a droplet of LSD on each woman's wrist. "Lick it up," said Eddie. "The rest will seep through your skin. Faye, you take the bathroom, Bunny the living room, I'll change in the bedroom. We'll begin in exactly ten minutes. Here's your uniform, Bunny."

Bunny looked through the pile of clothes. "God, I can't believe we still—it's our tenth anniversary?"

"Yes, well, it's our tenth meeting, but we began fifteen years ago. Remember, Bunny?"

Bunny smiled. "How could I forget? Bloomers?"

"Oh, aren't they—damn! Wait." Eddie hurried into the bedroom and hurried back clutching a pair of navy-blue gym bloomers. "Here they are. God, Bunny, I forget everything nowadays. Faye remembered the Bulletins or we'd be right in the middle of it without them. Do you think it's the marijuana? I've noticed my breasts are getting bigger too."

"No, Eddie. Only men's breasts get bigger from dope. They never said anything about *women's* breasts getting any bigger."

"No? That's odd. Naturally I just assumed. . . . I wonder why not?" Eddie shook her head and left the living room for the bedroom.

For the next nine minutes, silence blew like a gust of wind through Edda Mallory's apartment. Except for the thud of an occasional shoe, the rustle of cloth, a faucet running and then not, the clink of a cosmetic brush against a water glass, refrigerator purr, and distant high-heel clicks from the carpetless hall outside, there was no sound from any of the women, as was usual.

When exactly nine minutes had elapsed, Faye O'Jones was looking at herself in the mirror on the bathroom door and marveling at how well her Brearley uniform still fit. "Exactly as when I was there," she thought, "exactly the same. Which probably means that very little has happened since then to change me. What a terrifying thought." She took one last look at her long slim frame, her tiny, loafered feet, the navy knee socks, the navy U-necked gym tunic with pleated skirt ending just above the knee, and the white blouse with circle pin on left lapel. She smiled contentedly at her perfectly oval Unicorn Tapestry face, patted her Buster Brown hairdo only recently coiffed by Raymond & Nasser of West Fifty-seventh Street, and removed the pitch pipe from her purse. She turned the knob of the bathroom door and, as it opened, blew a C.

In the bedroom, Edda Mallory picked up the note and hummed it. It was time to begin. Eddie finished fastening the heart-shaped gold studs in her pierced earlobes and then stepped back from the mirror. Her heart-shaped face was serene, her great, round eyes a bit glazed with dope and wine, and her boot-black hair flowed straight as a Moonie's from the sharply pointed widow's peak in the center of her forehead. "I have never looked good in knee socks," she sighed, glancing at her childlike legs, "and I never will. Some things do not improve with maturity, they only get worse." Edda resumed humming, straightened her uniform, and opened the bedroom door. She joined Faye in the hall, and, humming in harmony, they entered the living room.

Bunny, also in uniform, and, by this time, also humming, rose from the couch as they entered, and joined them in a line. Faye blew the pitch again, and the three thirty-year-old women clothed in their old high school uniforms began to sing their old school song:

> "We're Brearley born,
> We're Brearley bred.
> And when we die,
> We're Brearley dead.
> So, rah, rah, for Brearley,
> Rah, rah for Brearley,
> Rah, rah for Brearley,
> Rah, rah, rah."

Their soprano voices melded for a moment, and then broke apart as, doing descant now, they surrounded the sofa. Each woman picked up her own aged Brearley bookbag and like a possessive mother cat, carried it to a preordained corner of the living room, opened it and began to remove the contents. Eddie, as grandmistress of the evening, paused by the tape player just long enough to hit the ON button and flood the living room with the uplifting strains of "The Theme from *2001.*" And like those cinematic hominids, who in slow motion discovered tool use, so each of the former Brearley girls, in slow motion and underscored by the music, extracted from her Brearley bookbag and held aloft a perfect eight-inch replica of a male penis. Tying on by means of leather thongs, beautifully and intricately carved of light beige pearwood by Bonita "Bunny" Warburton in 1962, the three fake phalluses hovered in the air and stayed there rather arrogantly until the music was over. The women then lowered them, tied them on like chaps, and began the meeting.

"My God, Bunny," said Faye, stroking her phallus lovingly, "you know you carved these when Jack Kennedy was still alive?"

"Did I?" asked Bunny plaintively. "Did I really? So long ago?"

"Things were so different then." Eddie lit the candles. "No boutiques, no pantyhose . . ."

"No birth-control pills, no body language . . ." Faye picked up an Alumnae Bulletin, ruffled through the pages, and set it back down. Bunny poured her another Scotch and from her purse retrieved the nutmeg and sprinkled it on top. Then she poured herself and Eddie some wine.

"No open marriage, no high-heeled boots, no discothèques, no pantsuits. Two orgasms under God, divisible." Once again Eddie hit the ON button and the voice of Bunny, age fifteen, filled the room.

BUNNY
(AGE 15)

And now . . . and now . . . c'mon, you guys, stop laughing or we can't do this. It's sacred, important. (Sounds and snorts from Faye and Eddie trying to calm down.) Okay. Okay. Now. We've known each other since we entered The Brearley as "Bs" some twelve years ago. We've been through a lot together.

FAYE AND EDDIE
(AGE 15)

Like what?

BUNNY

Like the getting of periods. When it happened, you remember, you were sitting, as was usual for you, on the knees of the god as on a cuddly Santa Claus at Macy's. Looking upward with your great big eyes, you were saying wistfully, "I'd really like a baby doll that cries real tears, or maybe one that talks if that's not too expensive," and suddenly your blood ran, well, not cold but hot and sticky and the togas of the gods were stained forever.

FAYE

Ah, puberty.

BUNNY

Call it by whatever name you want, missy. Our foreheads are scarred with the disappointments of it.

EDDIE

In the wearing of the Phalli, what we seek is understanding of our lot and theirs.

FAYE

Boys seem happier. Are they?

BUNNY

They seem stronger. Are they?

EDDIE

Simpler, well directed. Clarity helps a lot.

BUNNY

Is it in the Phallus?

FAYE AND EDDIE

Is it? Is it?

The three women, listening to the old tape, drinking, and feeling the acid kick in under their skin, looked down at their guest genitals and murmured in unison, "Is it? Is it?" The tape continued:

FAYE
If we don't get married and have children, is there a point to our lives, is there? I hate being a woman. I just hate it.

EDDIE
You're too intelligent to be one, Faye, that's all. Isn't it cruel that God gives intelligent women small breasts when clearly large sexy breasts would make life so much easier for them?

Eddie flipped off the tape. "My God, nothing's changed. I still think that and it's been fifteen years. Okay. You two sit down on the sofa. Go on."

Eddie gave Bunny and Faye a playful push in the direction of the couch. The two women, slightly unsteady, made it to the coffee table and set down their drinks. Their wooden penises bobbed up and down as they tottered to the sofa and flopped onto the overstuffed cushions. Bunny, without thinking, tried to cross her legs.

"Oh, I forgot," she said, and then, "Ow!" as the wooden shaft bumped her thigh. "You can't cross your legs. It's in the way. 'Course our fake ones are erect all the time. Perhaps it's different when it's flaccid."

"No," said Faye, "not very. They still feel it when their legs are crossed. Especially the testes."

"Well . . ." Bunny reached slowly for a joint and slowly lit it. "We wouldn't know about them."

"God, you don't trust your imagination, do you?" asked Eddie.

"Methinks the lady doth pretend too much. Let's not be hubristic, Eddie," Bunny pouted. "But it is true, it is true that they're always conscious of their penises. They have to be. That much"—she patted her phallus—"we've learned."

"Yes sir," agreed Faye emphatically. "From the moment I strap this on, I can't take my mind off it. What a burden it is hanging out there in the way all the time. It could get hurt, you know. I always worry about that. I once dated a guy who wore a metal athletic cup day and night, as a matter of course. I thought he was a paranoid macho asshole. Now I understand him. You know mine . . ." Faye peered down at her phallus. "Mine has a few nicks in it just from our meetings. I'm not kidding."

"I know exactly what you mean," said Eddie. "It's a real conversation stopper. It absorbs all your attention. I can't gossip when I'm wearing mine or talk about clothes. I become strong and silent. Everything seems unimportant except castration. Even rape."

"Last week a guy tried to rape me," said Bunny. The others gasped. "I told him I gave at the office. He believed me."

"Men don't perform sex acts with girls who wear contacts," countered Faye.

"I don't know why they say women aren't funny. Every time a man dresses up like one he gets a laugh," said Eddie, and the three women fell silent for a while, contemplating their phalluses.

"I think I have crotch rot," said Bunny finally. "Anyone have any gentian violet?"

"I'd like a Bud myself," said Faye. "Want a brew, Eddie?"

"No, but I would like some ballpark figures on a few things, if you guys don't mind. Bunny: At last count in your life you had had sex with forty guys?" Edda picked up a checklist and pen from the coffee table.

"Fifty now," said Bunny. Edda made a note.

"Faye, it was twenty-five?"

"Thirty."

"Me was thirty-five, now forty. You know I can't remember all their names anymore?"

"Last month I met one I had actually forgotten about." Faye clutched at her phallus. "Can you imagine? Surprised myself. Couldn't remember his name or where I'd met him even. We're getting old . . ."

"Hey, we're thirty. We're in our bloody prime and don't forget it!" Bunny spoke in a northern English accent. "If I were a man, I'd like to be Albert Finney."

"Why?" asked Faye. "I mean, I'd like to sleep with him, of course, but . . ."

"I don't know. He seems happy, doesn't he? Uncluttered. Bearlike."

"Yeah, but I'd like to be Alain Delon," said Eddie, pursing her lips to imitate his pouty mouth.

"Wanting to be Alain Delon," said Faye snippily, "is like wanting to be Frank Sinatra only French."

"Of course you read that in a fan magazine," Eddie sneered. "You don't know shit about Alain Delon's real life."

"It's common knowledge he's a gangster, Eddie, for Christ . . ."

"Well, who do you want to be?" asked Bunny.

"And living, Faye, living," said Eddie archly, "no dead Irishmen, okay?"

"For your information, the best Irishmen are dead Irishmen, but be that as it may, I'd like to be . . . Jerzy Kosinski."

"How odd," murmured Eddie to herself and blushed. She would have said more, but at that moment the acid kicked in fast and close and there was no more reason to speak.

Bunny, however, was floored. "Jerzy Kosinski?" She couldn't believe it. "*The Painted Bird* Kosinski? *Cockpit* Kosinski?" Faye nodded solemnly. "What does that mean, Faye? What does it mean to want to be Kosinski?"

"I don't know. I guess it means I want to be mysterious, literary, and kinkily macho. What's wrong? Did you want me to choose a fairy?"

"Of course not, but Kosinski's so esoteric, perhaps even domineering."

"If I want to be Kosinski, I can be Kosinski. Finis."

" 'Course you can, Faye. Sorry. Are you going under?"

"Not yet. Are you?"

"No, and I can tell it won't be fierce this time. Shall I give my report first?"

Eddie nodded. "Yes," said Faye, "go ahead."

Bunny rose from the sofa and made her way to the middle of the room. Edda, still silent and bubbling, sat down next to Faye and focused on Bunny.

Bonita "Bunny" Warburton, age thirty, stood before her two girlfriends from childhood wearing her old faded Brearley uniform and over it an erect eight-inch wooden phallus. She sighed deeply. Then she trotted to the coffee table, picked up a joint, and after lighting it, said,

"This acid's cut with speed. I know it. I can always tell."

"It's the coke," said Faye.

"Oh . . . maybe . . . it's possible." Bunny looked down at her phallus, grabbed it and, standing like a man who is peeing by the side of the road, began.

"Billy Dusenberg is, even as we speak, bald." Faye and Eddie gasped.

"Yes, the man on whose penis our own were modeled and carved some fifteen years ago is now forty-eight years old. I saw him on the street in Rome and nearly died. This was not the same young god we watched through the air vent of my parents' bathroom on East Eighty-fourth Street. I remember very clearly how beautiful he was, showering and soaping himself until he came."

Faye and Edda murmured in assent. Bunny, staring into memory as she talked, dreamily pulled at her wooden pud.

"I wish I hadn't seen him. I don't like reality much, as you know. For example, it's curious, but typical of me, that when I carved the phalluses, I looked through the air vent night after night, sometimes with you both, sometimes alone, noted every detail of the male shaft, every cord and vein . . . perfect. I was into Leonardo da Vinci at the time, but in the end, when I carved them, I forgot completely about the testicles. Or blocked them. At any rate, left them out. It's fitting that we've had no balls, that we've had to imagine them, invent them for ourselves. That's what it's all been about, I think, anyway."

"Bald," muttered Edda and Faye sadly and shook their heads.

"Yes. I'm sorry, but I had to tell you." Bunny bent over and touched her toes. On the way up she did a long isometric stretch to remove the tension from her neck. Over the years, she reminded her childhood friends alternately of Peter Pan and Wendy, depending on her mood, and often of Tinkerbelle. She was unearthly in her kindness but not cloying, and except for the meetings, at which she felt safe, she never got angry. When circumstances overwhelmed her, which they frequently did, she either blocked them out or fled. She made up charming stories to explain her disappearances, but they were all just trapped-rat fantasies. The meetings were the only times she ever told the truth.

"In accordance with the rules," she began, "I have told no one else of this adventure, nor will I ever tell. I have changed no names, for there are no innocents, except, of course, for me.

"Having escaped the villa, as I told you, I determined to seek out the tiniest, most inaccessible island I could find, a place where Arto could not find me, and where I could hide out until I was back in one piece. I found Antiparos. Deep in the Cyclades, a pimple of land a quarter of an hour by boat from Paros, it housed an ancient island community, population three hundred in winter, six hundred and fifty in summer.

"There was one main street along which all the houses were built, and sandwiched in between them, the shops: the wine shop—Parian wine, the kind Lawrence Durrell so dearly loves, and with good reason—the bakery, the meat shop, and the sweet shop. At one end of the street was the harbor, at the other, a minute main square, stark white and shaded by a huge plane tree. In one corner of the square sat a round, white church with a cross on top and a cross-eyed Byzantine saint in mosaic on the floor inside, in another, the bar where the old men bought and drank their ouzo.

In the summer there, the sun was like a golden gift. It spilled over on the squat, white houses with their aqua deco doors, and in the shadows it created, there was peace. The glare from this sun was so white that it burned away my memory and it melted all my fear. I was like a child again, but like no child I had ever been."

"Uh oh," said Eddie.

"Uh oh," chorused Faye.

Bunny twirled around, her phallus bobbing, and struck an adventurous pose, her arms open wide for emphasis.

"It was in this state that I deflowered the baker," she said gravely. Faye and Edda gasped. "Go on," they said. "Go on."

"I rented a room in the side of a house, a simple room with a bed, a chair, a table, and a picture of a Byzantine madonna on the wall. Over the lintel of my door was a grapevine which promised fruit, and on the earth outside, chickens chatted or fought among themselves—it's hard to tell the difference.

"I kept to myself at first, doing the odd woodcarving, contemplating my future, eating one meal at the harbor *taverna* and going to bed at seven. Anything to avoid contact with men. Anything to avoid trouble.

"And then one evening I stopped in at the bakery and I saw him."

Eddie pushed the button of the tape player:

FAYE, EDDA, AND BUNNY
(AGE 15)

WAS HE DARK OR WAS HE LIGHT?
WAS HE BIG OR WAS HE LEAN?
WAS HE DUMB OR WAS HE BRIGHT?
WAS HE NICE OR WAS HE MEAN?

Eddie pushed PAUSE. Bunny spoke in a wistful tone.

"He was covered in flour, hunched over a wooden table near a huge medieval-looking mixer. He was rhythmically kneading phyllo pastry. He was making *spanakopites*."

"Jesus," murmured Faye and Eddie.

"He was young," Bunny continued, "and tall and lean and blond and so filled with kinetic energy that he moved with the staccato excitement of an animal at play. As I entered the shop, he whipped around and stared at me from beneath white, floury eyelashes. He was naked to the waist, but wearing an apron and covered with this fine white powder like a tribesman in some fragile culture that will soon be wiped out.

"His first expression was one of surprise, and then he smiled and his features were filled with such complete and utter joy that my reserve fell round my ankles like a loose pair of panties. I moved toward him and he extended his pastry-covered hand and spoke the only English words he knew. 'Hello,' he said. 'Me: Apollo. You?' 'Bunny,' I replied."

"Apollo," said Eddie. "He was a god."

"With feet of dough," said Bunny, and her eyes filled up with tears.

"What is it, Bunny?" asked Faye gently.

"I don't know. I don't feel secure unless I'm married," she answered.

"I don't feel secure unless I'm not married," offered Eddie.

"I don't feel secure unless they're married," ended Faye. The three women laughed.

Bunny hiked up her imaginary nuts and continued.

"For three days we flirted like teenagers. The bakery became my malt shop. Invisible bobby sox adorned my feet. And then one night, he invited me to the open-air disco at the end of the island to eat a rabbit he had killed with a giant slingshot. And to watch him dance.

"There were long tables under the stars and a jukebox playing island songs. The bunny, barbecued and charred, lay stiff on the plates in juiceless rigor mortis. As I watched, four heavenly young men rose from their chairs, led by my Apollo, and glided to the dance floor. Slowly, very slowly, as if winding from the earth, they grasped each other's shoulders and began a dance as old as art. With long, unbending legs, Apollo held his brother's hand and flipped over and over like the wheel of a donkey cart on an island hill. He leapt and knelt and juggled chairs and tables and all the life his culture trapped within him crackled forth like lightning.

"That night, he walked me to my little room and we made love beneath the Byzantine madonna."

"And was he good?" the women asked.

"I was as filled with desire as I have ever been before or since," she answered.

"But was he good?" they asked again.

"He killed a bunny and he came like one. But he was so large that I forgave him for it. I chalked it up to Third World technical ignorance."

The women nodded in understanding.

"For two more days we were in love, and then he changed. Overnight, like a weather kitty from pink to blue, and I didn't have the language to ask him why." Bunny paused a moment to watch a tear drip off her cheek and onto her circle pin. Then she went on.

"Durrell was right. Things are never what they seem in Greece. The average person could have written *Rashomon*. Where there should have been smiles, there was icy detachment. Where there should have been pleasure was a vacuum of pain.

"I determined to learn Greek so I could find out what had happened. I sat beneath my grapevine and studied and studied. I memorized my paradigms till I had them down and then some. One evening I saw some young German men, drunken tourists, goose-stepping down the main street in the moonlight. The omenlike quality of the event filled me with foreboding. I shrank into the shadows and bumped into Ianni, a young college student who was learning English and had come to practice it on me.

" 'Bunny,' he said, wringing his hands with much disgust, 'I don't know words to say this, but I try. Apollo tells everything you do at night. He laughs about you with the pals. He is bad, Bunny. He is . . .' He used the word for 'crude.'

"I was so embarrassed, girlfriends, and so shocked, that for a moment, my soul actually left my body and hovered above it—as in situations where people have almost died, same thing. I suffered in that instant a kind of emotional death and then— I laughed."

"Bravo," yelled Eddie.

"Bravo," yelled Faye.

"Give 'em humor, Bunny, give it to 'em!" they yelled together.

"In the cheeriest of moods I denied it all: love, sex, flirtation, everything. And, having no experience of women, Ianni believed me. I sent him on his way to plead my case, and off he went.

"Apollo still came to me at night and I still made love with him, I'm not sure why. In some strange way I was biding my time, spinning the web of words with which I could finally have my say. A say I could never have with Arto, or my father, or my mother. The release of my body meant little in return for the release of mind I would finally effect.

"Old Theodoros came to warn me too. This toothless fisherman, age ninety-five, laughing and dancing in senility, part weathered grandpapa, part *commedia dell'arte* clown, brought me fruit and, pressing his gnarled hands in prayer, rolled his eyes heavenward and moaned, 'Bad boys. You watch.' Then he tried to kiss me and scampered out the door.

"My resolve was set. The episode was drawing to a close. As was the summer weather. Arto's yacht had been sighted in Paros and the island was no longer safe for me. Ianni was returning to Athens by the next boat, and I would go with him. The night before our departure, Apollo came to my room one last time. The moment had arrived.

"I had a speech prepared. A good one too. Phrases from

Cavafy and Homer, epithets of outrage from the street, but I never got to give it. Because when I asked why, why were you so mean, the opening salvo, he hung his head and cried. 'Because I was a virgin, Bunny. Because I was afraid.' 'You've never had a woman before?' I had to make sure. 'No,' he answered simply. I crumpled up my speech and threw it to the chickens. My only regret is that I left before the grapes had ripened."

"Isn't that always the way?" said Eddie.

"Bunny, what a coup!" said Faye.

"And how bizarre," mused Bunny. "I deflowered him and he treated me badly. Can you believe it? No woman would do that. Would she?"

"*No!*" the women had no doubts.

"So I won," Bunny went on, "without knowing it. I expect he'll never forget me. You always remember the first one."

"Don't remind me," said Faye.

"It was sad, actually. He said he was afraid he'd fall in love and then I'd leave and he'd be heartbroken. So instead he ruined my reputation in the village and almost got my head shaved. What a jerk. But my revenge was in the fact of having sex with him. I mean, I'm an experienced American woman. A repressed Greek girl's going to have to go some to top me."

"Definitely," agreed Faye.

Edda took up the checklist. "Anal sex?" she asked, pencil poised.

"No, no," said Bunny, "I save that for my husbands. But everything else. I was in love. I told you."

"You really couldn't tell he was a virgin?" asked Faye.

"No. I guided him in as I always do, *et voilà*, he plunged like all the rest."

"Did you feel powerful when you found out?" asked Eddie.

"Very powerful, Eddie. Magical almost. And dumb, really dumb."

"Wait a minute," said Eddie, "something's wrong here. I

can't believe that this guy was locker-rooming all over the island and you didn't do something."

Bunny smiled. "I never should have shared my frog with you in Biology X."

"Well?" the women asked.

"Well," Bunny admitted, "there was one olive-skinned, black-eyed, perfectly formed, young sailor with whom I dallied on the sly. He wore a silver bullet from Cyprus around his neck. I couldn't resist."

"Bravo, Bunny," Faye and Edda applauded. "Great report."

Bunny did a low curtsy and pretended to almost poke her eye out with her phallus. The women howled and Bunny collapsed on the floor.

"All right, ladies." Faye imitated their sixth-grade homeroom teacher: "Quieten down."

"Do you have an imitation for us?" asked Eddie.

"Okay, yes, but I need some coke first." Bunny went to the coffee table and snorted two lines. She loitered for a moment, feeling it kick against the acid, and then when she felt it lift her up out of the ooze, she returned to the center of the room and faced her friends.

Like a cat interested in something funky, Bunny stretched out her neck and sniffed exaggeratedly at the head of her wooden pecker. Her girlfriends roared. Then with a perplexed expression, she gave it a few short licks and then looked even more perplexed. They laughed more.

"Okay," she began, "I am going to do my husband, Arto Veneziano, Italian financier, age thirty-seven. The speech that made me flee the villa. *Buono.* He's a big man, Arto, heavyset, stands up real straight like Benito Mussolini." Bunny drew herself up until her back was ramrod-straight, her nose up in the air, and an arrogant holier-than-thou mask claimed her face. Her big, stiff penis protruded from her groin as if it owned the airspace around it. In profile she looked like an obscene pouter pigeon.

"Ah, you laugh." Bunny spoke in a deep voice with a heavy Italian accent. "American women are so hard, so demanding. They do not have the gentleness, the wish to comfort a man, to soothe him." She gestured with cupped fingers, a pained expression shadowing her face and passing into condescension, grabbing occasionally at her phallus for emphasis. "I do not ask the earth of you, Bunny, just that you open your mind a little. You are no longer an innocent little child. You are a thirty-year-old-woman, though in certain lights you hardly look it, *cara.*

"Can you not do this one tiny thing for your Arto? Such a little thing to make an old man happy? The costume is stupendous, worth a fortune, the gleaming feathers of a thousand tropical birds—all illegal to import and kill, but done so at my request, for you, because it is my whim. Costumed thus, as a new and glorious phoenix, I will place you in a giant birdcage made of golden filigree fashioned by Arab friends in Agadir, and there you'll stay chirping and fluttering aboard a golden trapeze until our anniversary party is over. If we don't make Italian *Vogue* with this, we cancel our subscription, *pronto.*"

Bunny strutted about and then continued. "It's magnificent, Bunny, the whole fantasy, and I really don't see how you raise objections of this vulgar women's lib when I am talking of surrealism. Not only is it beneath you intellectually but it hurts me. You are my little bird, Bunny, and the golden cage is symbolic of our love and how I want you. Please do not throw away all we have had together for some women's group's principle of life. Ah, by the way, *cara,* within the cage, you will find a new caftan. Woven of golden thread and beaded with semiprecious stones, it is yours for doing me this one wifely . . . duty."

Bunny adjusted the crotch of her imaginary trousers and, miming Arto's goosestep, left the room.

"Jesus Christ," said Eddie.

"For really and truly?" asked Faye.

"Umhumm," answered Bunny as she strolled back into the living room. "I need more acid. I didn't get off." She picked up the Visine bottle and dabbed two drops of liquid behind her ears.

"Hey, be careful, now that I'm not screwing Kundalini Ken it's a lot harder to get that stuff out of him. Limited supply, definitely not for use when bitter." Eddie took the bottle from Bunny.

"I'm sorry," murmured Bunny weakly and headed for the couch.

"Psychedelic, though, Bunny," said Faye, getting up. "Very psychedelic guy, Arto. You have had a year. Sit down, kiddo. These men are exhausting. It's my turn, I think. Let me fix myself a Scotch and I'll proceed."

Faye poured herself a drink and sprinkled it with nutmeg. She took a few sips and then carried the glass to the center of the room, faced Eddie and Bunny, and began.

"I'd like to propose a toast." Faye raised her glass. "To our tenth anniversary. I wonder if we'll still be doing this when we get married—if we get married. Don't get me wrong, I'm very glad to be wearing my phallus again. Frankly, I've missed the old dick." Faye looked fondly at her imitation manhood and patted the tip. "Excuse my *crudité*. There are times when I'm alone when I'm simply dying to strap it on, to calm myself down and get another perspective. Does anyone else feel like that? It kind of worries me."

Eddie and Bunny nodded. "I'd like to wear it while I write," confessed Eddie. "I have this feeling that if I wore it while writing, I'd have more confidence and use less adjectives. It's okay Faye-o. It's just fantasy. Don't worry about it."

"Okay," Faye sighed and drank her Scotch. "It's just we never talk about stopping, you know, or maybe graduating's a better word, and I have this picture of us at eighty, stooped over and doddering, still wearing these by-then-petrified dildoes, and it's weird."

"Of course it's weird, Faye." Bunny was getting off on the acid and this was her last verbal assay. "It was weird when we were fifteen, it's weird now and it'll be really weird if at eighty we still have incidents to report."

"We'll stop when it's time, Faye. I think we'll all know when, and that will be it. But, of course," Eddie glanced down at her phallus, "any girl who wants to stop now can do so."

"No, no." Faye put down her drink. "I'm sorry. It's been a while. I'm between boyfriends and a little cranky. Momentary drug paranoia. I went with it. I apologize. Okay. Big treat. My report is entitled 'The Massage Parlor,' and, yes, I bought a man for sex."

Edda pushed the ON button of the tape player.

FAYE, EDDA, AND BUNNY
(AGE 15)

WAS HE DARK OR WAS HE LIGHT?
WAS HE BIG OR WAS HE LEAN?
WAS HE DUMB OR WAS HE BRIGHT?
WAS HE NICE OR WAS HE MEAN?

Edda pushed PAUSE. Faye spoke in a sarcastic tone.

"He was very hard to find. Most hustlers in this town are either women or gay."

"But he was straight?" asked Eddie.

"He was straight, all right." Faye seemed upset at the memory. Her friends braced themselves. It happened. All the stories weren't pretty. That was part of the pact: They didn't have to be. And if they weren't, nobody blamed the woman who told them. Rule No. 4 said it clearly: "Just because you have a weird experience doesn't make you weird." It was because of this rule and others like it that the women kept on meeting. It was the only place on earth they didn't have to mind their P's and Q's.

Faye O'Jones was very beautiful with her slim, model's body and her deep-red Buster Brown hair. She was a classicist and a

physical anthropologist with a Ph.D. from the University of
Chicago. She was as well educated as a woman could get, and
as socially prominent, and yet there was a hardness in her that
seemed misplaced in one so perfect. She attributed it to a trace
of white trash she once found in her family tree. "Irish scum,"
she joked. But her close friends knew it was a terror of sex, not
because she told them, but because they were women too and
they just knew. They were at a loss how to help her.

"What a great idea, Faye O'," said Edda.

"Yes," said Faye, stroking her phallus and staring into space
as she spoke, "I just wanted to have some sex, you know. Get
off." She pushed her pelvis forward obscenely. "Get my end
wet. Pop the big cork. I wanted to buy a hooker and get serviced. A guy who wouldn't judge me. The freedom to release
the tension in my body without a big production. Do you
understand?"

"Do we understand?" the women shouted. "Do we understand!"

"Okay," Faye continued. "I heard about this massage parlor
in the Commodore Hotel that had guys who serviced women. I
called up and made an appointment. Fifty dollars for hot-oil
massage, champagne bubble bath, fingertip powder rub. Anything else—extra. I would have to ask. How do you ask? Do
you come right out with it? Are there code words? Are men
born knowing these things? Or what?"

"Or what?" Eddie and Bunny chorused. "Or what?"

"It was a place that catered to men and women. The en-
tranceway was round, which I liked. I paid my money and was
escorted by a bubbly young woman in a red leotard and black
net stockings, into a room with some black leather couches and
a bar at one end. Several other young women, also clad in
leotards, offered me a drink, and when I accepted, scurried off
to get it."

"Excuse me," said Eddie and leaned forward. "What did you
wear to this event?"

"Good question. It wasn't easy choosing an outfit, I can tell you. Black tee shirt, black trousers, black suede jacket, black boots, dark glasses—the mirrored aviator kind. I looked like a hitter girl from Vassar. I was nervous, I admit it. The women were all very pretty, young, under twenty-five, and filled with bouncy good humor. They seemed to enjoy their job at the massage parlor and after they brought me my drink, they perched all together on one of the couches, smiling lazily, a profusion of full lips, big eyes and slender arms, like a pile of lizards on a Galápagos island. A businessman entered the room now, as I had, glanced around nervously, saw me and asked if he could buy me a drink. The mound of women laughed and a mouth said, 'She's here for the same purpose as you.' More giggles. The businessman blushed.

"At the other end of the room, a gaunt, wimpy young man with acne, glasses, and a breast-pocket pencil case murmured through painful shyness, 'New Jersey and I just don't get along,' to the girl in the red leotard who nodded sympathetically and encouraged him in his story. I turned away to look at my watch and the girl in red suddenly screamed. The mound of women froze, heads and eyes snapping toward the danger like a tableau of frightened antelopes when a lion is near. The wimpy young man was writhing on the floor. He was having an epileptic fit. Through the contortions on his face, the full scope of his vulnerability was laid bare. Of all the places, of all the times . . . The manager appeared swiftly and carried the young man off to a back room. 'I was going to put my bag in his mouth,' said the girl in red. The mound of women, all wide eyes and open mouths, sighed in relief.

"I got up to leave. All I needed was to be arrested in a midtown massage parlor. Can you see me ringing Mummy for bail? The manager stopped me. 'Come this way,' he said. It was he I had purchased for the afternoon.

"The man was tall and well-built, in his early thirties, curly hair and a mustache, good-looking in the way of guys who frequent discos or singles bars. Not my usual type. Not a criminal musician, not a preppie with good brain and a screwed-up sexuality. Not at all.

"He led me through the same door through which he had carried the epileptic, into a dimly lit corridor. I followed him along this silent and airless passageway, fearing, curiously, not for my life, but for my youth, as if what I was about to do would somehow take it from me. It was guilt, of course, and old morality. Nothing changes you unless you let it. Even bad sexual experiences. Even good ones.

"We hurried into a black room, with a black leather massage table and pink neon lighting. The manager, Mr. Singles Bar I'll call him, smiled and said in a soft, deep voice, 'We'll be in here.' He bade me get undressed and then disappeared through a side door down another corridor.

"As I removed my clothes, which wasn't easy, let me tell you, I was shaking with anxiety, telling myself to relax and enjoy it—a man would, for God's sake. Get your money's worth. The manager returned." Faye ran to her Brearley bag and removed from it a small towel, which she secured around her waist like a miniskirt. The wood pecker bulged against the terry cloth. Faye went on.

"He was wearing"—she modeled it—"a small towel. Which, frankly, I found undignified, if not presumptuous. But I guess there's only so much time. You can't dawdle. I was nude, lying on the table, desperately trying to fantasize something. He began to massage me and as he did so, he asked me questions: Where was I from? What did I do? Why did I do it? Everything but why was I there, which was what he really wanted to know.

"Of course I told him nothing. I was wondering how to ask for 'extras.' Do you offer money first? Do you not mention money 'cause that's weird? Are men born knowing these things or is it always all right to be rude to a hooker?"

"The latter," the women interjected. "A man can treat a prostitute like dirt under his feet. It's the law."

"Well . . ." Faye scratched her phallus through the towel. "It doesn't work the other way. I was afraid he'd yell at me if I asked him wrong. Or hit me, you know?"

"We know. We know." The women smiled ruefully. Eddie pushed the ON button of the tape player.

FAYE, EDDA, AND BUNNY
(AGE 15)
ON MY POWER, I WILL TRY
TO DO MY DUTY TO DAD AND MY COUNTRY,
TO HELP OTHER PEOPLE MOST TIMES OF
THE MONTH
AND TO OBEY THE GIRL SPROUT LAWS.

Edda pushed PAUSE. Faye continued.

"Finally I got my courage up. So far, the massage was terrible, too soft. There's a German lady at the Health Club for Women in the Ritz Tower who is far superior. Anyway. Mr. Singles Bar was fingertipping around my nipple. I looked up at him and in my most girlish voice I asked, 'Do you do any extras?'

" 'What extras?' he asked coquettishly. I blushed.

" 'Foreplay,' I muttered.

" 'Cunnilingus?' he asked, smiling.

"I breathed a sigh of relief. I wouldn't have to say it.

" 'Yes,' I replied, eyes tightly closed.

" 'No,' he said simply. 'No. I never do cunnilingus with clients. I have to draw the line somewhere. I save that for the women I love.' "

"*Oh no!*" Bunny and Eddie wailed. "*Oh no!*"

"I sat up. 'What?' I said. I couldn't believe it. 'No cunnilingus? Just my luck.'

" 'No,' he said again, never with clients. I'm no weirdo, I have my pride.'

" 'But do you really do it with the women you love?' I asked.

"He turned away. 'I will when I find Miss Right,' he said wistfully. 'I'm not sure I'm capable of love.'

" 'I see,' I said and thanked him for the massage.

" 'Is that all you want?' he seemed surprised.

" 'Yes, that's all, thanks.' I got off the table and began to dress. 'Yes, thanks. That's all.' He nodded and made for the side door.

" 'I'm going through some changes right now. You understand?' he asked.

" 'Sure.' I waved to him as he left. 'I understand.' "

"Faye O', that's hilarious!" Eddie was preparing the opium for smoking. She got out a piece of tinfoil, a candle, and three straws and placed them on the coffee table. She lit the candle and dropped one of the opium balls onto the tinfoil. She handed Faye and Bunny the straws and held the foil over the candle so the flame was just beneath the opium. When it began to run, she cried, "Okay, Brearley girls, chase the dragon! Chase it. Chase it."

The women inhaled and held their breaths and then Eddie said, "Jesus. You can't even buy oral sex. You can't even buy it."

"If I ever have a son"—Faye exhaled and her voice was incredibly deep—cunnilingus will be his first word, bet on it."

"It's true"—Bunny exhaled—"women bring up their goddam sons to hate oral sex. What a travesty."

"Do you have your imitation, Faye?" asked Eddie.

"I do. Ladies, please welcome: Johnny Carson's proctologist." Faye whipped off the towel, and her phallus popped up cheerily. "No, just kidding. I'm doing the impostor. And frankly, the impostor will never let you down."

Faye adjusted some imaginary testicles and attempted to push down her phallus. It sprang up and she began.

"I met Ben on a horse in Central Park. He claimed to be the lead singer of the mediocre rock group Puss. He lived at the Navarro, and indeed his room was filled with costume trunks and musician's equipment. The picture on the album, which I checked out at Sam Goody's, was blurry but resembled him. I suspected he was an impostor, but until I read of his arrest in the *Daily News*, I wasn't sure. Here is an excerpt from our last night together."

Faye rounded her skinny shoulders, flexed her puny muscles, and tried to look like a bear of a man. She ran to her Brearley book bag and took from it a miniature football, which she then began tossing from hand to hand. She bent over like a player in a huddle and grunted, as her wooden penis bobbed against her chest. Clutching the football under her arm, she raised her head and addressed Eddie and Bunny.

"I had this with me in 'Nam," she said and shook her head. "Oh, not this"—she patted the phallus—"the football. Used to throw it around at Khe Sanh during the lulls. Kept it with me to the end, you know Faye, through everything, even when the guy next to me—" She gasped for breath, large noisy gulps that consumed her body and made her phallus wiggle in rhythm. "Excuse me, Faye." Gasp. Gulp. "Throw the football with me before bed, Faye, it's good for you. C'mon, girl, get that skinny body moving. Het hup. Het hup. Okay, you're defense and I'm coming through—first and ten at the ten, eight seconds left. I'm coming through. Run, girl, stop me, stop me, Faye."

Faye, impersonating the impersonator, ran forward hunched over, wildly dodging the imaginary defense that included herself. She was out of control, bobbing and stumbling, and finally fell to the floor screaming, "Touchdown! Touchdown!" She lay there wide-eyed and gasping for a moment and then said softly, "You know, Faye, you look Asian. Did anyone ever tell you that? 'Cause you do, Faye, you know, you really look Asian. So skinny and everything. They don't get enough to eat either, girl. You got some smack, Mamasan?"

"Jesus, Faye, you all right?" Eddie helped her up.

"Before sex," Faye said as she dusted herself off, "we always played football. Someone had to get a touchdown before we could go to bed. No field goals allowed—I tried once." Faye put the football back in her book bag.

"I slept with a Vietnam vet once," said Bunny. "Got my period and bled all over the sheets. Didn't faze him."

"Well, they're not all nuts, Bunny," said Faye, "only the ones I pick. Well, Eddie, I think it's your turn now. Where's that Scotch?"

"Why do you put nutmeg in your Scotch, Faye?" Eddie was chopping up the last of the cocaine and dividing it into lines. Bunny, who was now tripping heavily, watched the movements of the razor blade silently and with complete absorption.

"For effect and because it keeps people from noticing how much booze I drink. It gives it an air of cuteness it wouldn't ordinarily have."

With this, Faye lost her balance, careened onto the couch, and fell violently against Eddie, causing the razor blade in her hand to skidder off the heart-shaped mirror and into Bunny's lap, lodging finally at a punkish angle in Bunny's wooden phallus.

"Oh my God," screamed Eddie.

"I've castrated her," screamed Faye.

Bunny stared at her wounded phallus and began to cry. The downstairs buzzer rang insistently, and Eddie, in total confusion, ran to answer it.

"Oh my God, let me remove it, Bunny." Faye leaned over drunkenly and tried to pull out the razor blade. She was too drunk and stoned to dislodge it. Bunny just cried.

"Leave it, Faye, you'll cut yourself." Eddie hung up the intercom.

"Who was it?" asked Faye.

"I'm not sure." Eddie looked blank.

"What do you mean?"

"I'm really blitzed, Faye. I could be hallucinating."

"Well, who do you think it was?"

Eddie looked sheepish. "Jerzy Kosinski. I told him to come up." The doorbell rang, and the three women looked in the direction of the door.

"Do you know Jerzy Kosinski or is this some kind of Zen

miracle?" Faye had sobered up in about three seconds and was talking fast and furiously.

"Yes. My report's about him. It was a surprise."

The doorbell rang again, three short rings and a long, three short rings and a long.

"That's a code we have. He likes spy stuff."

"Are you saying that Jerzy Kosinski's at the door and we're here like this?" Faye was on her feet now, albeit weaving.

"You said you wanted to meet him." Eddie was staggering toward the door.

"I had hoped for more dignified circumstances, Edda—a literary cocktail party, the National Book Award luncheon, anything but this. Am I right, Bunny?"

Bunny nodded and continued weeping. Eddie turned the doorknob and Faye shouted in desperation, her hands shielding her phallus, "No men allowed, Eddie, never for fifteen years—what the hell are you doing—I said I wanted to *be* him, not meet him."

"I didn't ask him over, for God's sake, Faye, he just dropped by, like manna from heaven if you ask me, since everyone was talking about him all evening. He'll understand, Faye. This is child's play compared to war-torn Poland, you know what I mean?"

Eddie opened the door. Faye froze and Bunny stopped crying. Kosinski was startled.

"I thought you said you were alone, Eddie," he said with a heavy Eastern European accent. "I lied, Jerzy," Eddie replied matter-of-factly. "I'm here with two girlfriends. We're wearing our old private-school uniforms with wooden phalluses tied over them, and chatting about men."

"Ah, well, in that case." Kosinski strode quickly into the apartment and surveyed the scene. Eddie closed the door behind him. He made sure it was locked.

Faye looked up at the tall, skinny author with his hooked nose and his piercing pupilless black eyes and stammered, "I'm

terribly embarrassed, Mr. Kosinski. These, uh . . ." She pointed
to her phallus. "We—well, Bunny actually carved them and we
certainly never thought anyone else would see."

"No, please, I love it," said Kosinski, took off his coat and sat
down next to Bunny.

"Oh. Jerzy, that's Bunny Warburton next to you and F—"

"No names, Eddie," Faye interrupted desperately. "I had
thought I might meet you under more/less vulnerable circumstances, but fate was very unkind and I . . ."

"You look beautiful, if that's what you mean. May I?" Kosinski took Faye's phallus in his hands and examined it intently.

"You carved this, Bonny?"

"Bunny to you," said Bunny with hostility. She was verbal
again but wildly drugged and resented his intrusion. "You
really write *The Painted Bird*?"

"Yes."

"That stuff really happen to you?"

"Well, Bonny, there are always questions. Is there such a
thing as fact? Is there such a thing as fiction?"

"Yeah. Yeah. You see this?" Bunny grabbed her phallus.
"This is definitely fiction."

"On you a penis is fiction. On me it is fact. You see?"

"He keeps a comet in the back of his car. I've seen it," offered Eddie.

"Listen." Bunny grabbed Kosinski's coat by the neck and
with her face close to his, spoke to him through clenched teeth.
"Did you really see those peasants break a bottle inside that
retarded woman? 'Cause if you didn't I'm going to kill you. I
hate that scene. I hate it so much and it's frightening and
painful and ugly. And ever since I unsuspectingly read that, it
haunts me and comes back to me when I least suspect it. And
if you made that up, then you're a sick guy and I'm going to
kill you."

"No!" screamed Faye and pushed Bunny away. "Do you
know who this is? Do you know whom you're talking to?

Eddie, Bunny, it's the man with the pipe, the man I told you about at the party for the Rex in the museum."

"Your fiancé, Faye?" Eddie and Bunny looked at each other conspiratorially. Kosinski's eyes darted wildly.

"This jerk?" shouted the crazed Bunny. "This torturer of women? This avowed rapist is the man you love?"

"I see you've read all my books."

"Really, Bunny." Faye's voice was icy. "Mr. Kosinski is a distinguished author. I cannot allow you—"

"No, please, I love it." Kosinski smiled. "I have touched her. Readers often become angry with me. I am used to it."

"That's very gracious of you, Mr. Kosinski." Faye spoke haltingly and with great emotion. "I think you deserve an explanation."

"Yes, please. Tell me about the phalluses—when did you start wearing them? Why? Eddie, why didn't you let me know?" He scrutinized the coffee table and added, "My God, so many drugs. How does it work?"

"Oh, that," said Faye, disappointed. "I'm going to get that Scotch now. Like something, Mr. Kosinski?"

"No. No thank you."

"He doesn't do drugs. And he rarely drinks," said Eddie.

"Never," advised Bunny, "trust a man who doesn't get high. But don't necessarily trust one who does."

"Thank you, Bunny." Eddie was standing before Kosinski and Bunny, who were seated side by side on the sofa. Faye bustled in from the kitchen and took the seat on the other side of Kosinski.

"Okay Bunny, relax."

Eddie smiled at Kosinski.

"Let's see, Jerzy: This is our tenth anniversary of meeting together and wearing the phalluses, but actually we started doing this about fifteen years ago in high school, which is when Bunny carved them."

"But why? Why do you put on phalluses? What is the real

reason?" Kosinski was captivated. He was almost taking notes. Faye ran her fingers through his thick black hair.

"Penis envy," said Bunny, and with a violent wrench, she pulled the razor blade out of her phallus. She keened for a moment over the thing between her legs and then continued, "Simple classic penis envy. Could there be another reason?" She examined the wounded wood pecker to see what recarving she would have to do.

"Eddie, what do you say?" he asked.

"Sympathetic magic. Make a sound like lightning and it might rain."

"But how does it work?" he pressed. "Why do you put on your private-school uniforms? Why the drugs?"

Eddie considered this. "The uniforms—we used to wear the uniforms in high school, of course, and after that . . ." She turned to Bunny, who took up the explanation in annoyance.

"They remind us of a virginal state. I saw a movie once where Sophia Loren puts on a white dress and walks into the sea to commit suicide. After she's been promiscuous, of course. Sort of like that. Understand, Mr. K.? As The Brearley wisely pointed out, you have no status, past, or future in the uniform. No image. It's a leveling, egalitarian factor, dig? Like a crewcut."

"Ah." Kosinski smiled mischievously. "Sincerity. I see."

"You better believe it, buster!" Bunny saluted him. "As for the drugs, well, this is a sixties trio. We like drugs. They relax us after a hard year of dealing with guys." Bunny sat back and started whittling her phallus with the razor blade.

Eddie resumed speaking. "Anyway, Jerzy, we meet every three years or so and give reports about experiences we've had that have, uh, widened our horizons. Given us a glimpse of who we are and what we can endure. My report this year was on you. I'm not quite sure what to do now." Edda looked to Bunny, who shrugged uncaringly. Faye was snuggled up to Kosinski's neck with her eyes closed, possibly asleep.

"Please." Kosinski grinned in gleeful anticipation. "Give your report. I'd love to hear it."

"I bet," Bunny snapped. "Do it, Eddie. But if you do, don't soften it."

Faye sat bolt upright. "Don't do anything of the kind," she gasped. "You can't rip someone to shreds in front of him, Eddie, especially a man. They can't take it. It's bitchy and cruel and not necessary."

"I am dying to hear it, really," said Kosinski, and he was.

"We'll see about that," Bunny chuckled and sat back waiting for Eddie to begin. Faye took another swig of Scotch, dropped her head onto her chest and massaged the temples beneath her bangs.

Edda Millicent Mallory stood before the couch in her gym tunic and her phallus, her heart-shaped face flushed with some embarrassment and many drugs. Her great blue eyes twinkled with fear and lust, and the sharpness of her widow's peak made her look, she knew, like a depraved little angel. She stared at Kosinski and began.

"My report is entitled 'The Master Beater.' "

"Great title, Eddie," Kosinski said.

Eddie nodded.

"One night, at a fancy dinner party, I was seated next to a beautiful young socialite whose name often appears in the columns. About halfway through the meal, she suddenly turned to me and asked, 'Would you like to meet my friend Jerzy Kosinski?' I knew better than to ask for explanations so I simply said, 'Of course I would,' and gave her my card.

"I was afraid it wouldn't happen. It was a wish come true. Of course I'd read *The Painted Bird*—what sensitive, intellectual, inwardly submissive woman hasn't? And, of course, it had changed my life."

"It sure did," Bunny hissed at Kosinski. "What about that retarded woman? What about her?" She brandished the razor blade near his face. "Let's cut him." She grinned evilly. "Let's get some winos in here to sodomize him—what d'ya say?"

"Bunny!" Faye was horrified. She leaned over and extracted the razor blade from Bunny's fist and put it in her purse.

"Quiet, Bunny," said Edda and continued her tale.

"He called the next morning and arranged a lunch for the following Wednesday at one o'clock. I could hardly wait. I was thrilled. A date with Jerzy Kosinski—it's a Brearley girl's wet dream, let's face it. For you, Bunny, it'd be the equivalent of having a date with Edvard Munch, okay?"

Bunny nodded.

"Okay. The Wednesday of the lunch, I was so excited I could hardly stand it. The doorbell rang at noon—one hour early. It was Kosinski. He apologized but told me he had come an hour early to catch me unaware to see what I was really like. Little did he know, I'd been dressed and ready since nine A.M. But anyway, I was captivated.

"He was very mysterious. He checked my doors and windows to make sure they were locked and questioned me about the neighbors in the building across the way. He paced the floor like a caged panther and hissed so violently at a kitten I had just gotten that it didn't come out for the next three days. He was a sexy Scrooge, a gamin Raskolnikov. I was putty in his hands."

"Yes, yes you were, Eddie," Kosinski nodded happily.

"He took me out to lunch that day and dinner many times after, but at no time did he ever order anything himself. He told me he ate only enough to stay alive, and that at home. His favorite food is Mrs. Paul's frozen fish sticks."

"Mrs. Paul's fish sticks." Bunny turned to Kosinski. "Really and truly?"

"Yes," he replied, "I quite like them."

"God." She rolled her eyes in disgust.

"Shut up, Bunny, will you?" barked Faye. "Nobody cares what you think of Jerzy's favorite food." Faye was very angry.

"Oh, it's Jerzy now. Fast work, Faye. Not two minutes ago it was a thoroughly demure Mr. Ko—"

"Stop!" commanded Edda, her hands on her hips, her phallus trembling. "No fighting during my report. I continue.

"After our first meeting, he sent me everything he had written—a big package of books, pamphlets and magazine tearsheets which I read avidly. I was terribly impressed by the clarity of his mind and the energy that emanated from it. I am not ashamed to say that I wanted some of that clarity to rub off on me. I wanted some of that energy for my own. I wanted to sleep with him. But he refused."

"He *refused?*" Faye and Bunny couldn't believe it.

"Yes"—Edda blushed at the memory—"he refused. But he called me constantly and demanded my opinion of things. He praised my writing to the rafters and showered me with literary oddities he thought I should be exposed to. I demanded to have sex with him. But he refused."

"*Oh no!*" Faye and Bunny chorused.

"Yes." Edda stared menacingly at the gaunt author sandwiched between her high school chums. "Yes. He refused again. I was wild. Finally a man of such angst and savvy that he truly understood me! Finally a man who could match my intelligence and then some! A perverse child-adult just like me. Brutalized and abused at puberty, mute for seven years, what woman could resist such an obvious need for love? I pleaded to have sex with him."

"And did he refuse?" Faye and Bunny leaned forward with rapt attention. Edda let a few beats go by and tapped her phallus with her fingernail.

"No, this time he did not refuse." All three women looked at Kosinski. "This time he agreed.

"One night, about two months after we met, he brought me to a weird little apartment near Brearley. It was not his home, no, but something of a storage room for his toys. In the closet was a collection of nondescript military-type uniforms which he told me he used to assume false identities in situations where false identities were needed. He did not elaborate.

"In the main room was a sofa, which he unfolded and made up. I would have thrown over everything for him, even the Finchley porno-romance series, even Mrs. Bainbridge, everything. He removed from a drawer a black doctor's bag which he set carefully by the bed. I have never been so turned on in my life. He bade me get undressed and lie down with my arms and legs spread, which I did. He vanished momentarily and then reappeared clutching a handful of old club neckties: the Harvard Club, Yale, Princeton. And with these slim proclamations of status, he bound my wrists and ankles to the bedframe."

"Eddie"—Faye was chewing a nail anxiously—"I don't think you should go on with this. It's one thing if the man is not here, but under the circumstances . . ."

"Go on, Eddie." Kosinski was clearly delighted with the proceedings.

"Yeah," agreed Bunny. "Get to the good part!"

"All right." Edda shifted uneasily. "He removed from the doctor's bag a hand vibrator and a little black whip. And he—" Edda stopped. She thought for a moment and then ran to the bookcase and removed from it a copy of *Blind Date*, Kosinski's latest work. She flipped through the pages impatiently until she found page 230, the one she sought. "And then he . . ." She handed the open book to Bunny and pointed to a specific line midpage. Bunny took the book, leaned over Kosinski's lap and, with Faye, read the paragraph Edda had pointed out.

"He did that?" Bunny was shocked. So was Faye.

"Yes." Edda leaned over the sofa. "Only here, where the girl says 'Yes,' I said 'No' and broke the ties. Ripped them from the bedframe!"

"Good for you," said Bunny, outraged. "But what about the whip? There's no mention of the whip here."

"I know. But that's the whole thing, don't you see? He wrote about it but he told it differently. He left out the most important part."

"The vibrator," said Faye, "what did he do with the vibrator? Point it out." She held out the book and Edda pointed to a line.

Kosinski shook his head. "I never saw anything like it. She is a puritan, a direct descendant of the Mathers. I have told her so."

"You did this?" Faye asked Kosinski directly.

"I had to. She is terrified of orgasms. She had never had a real orgasm. I had to do something."

"That isn't true!" Edda stamped her foot and her phallus quivered.

"Well . . ." Kosinski threw up his hands.

"Why didn't you write about the vibrator and the whip?" demanded Eddie.

Faye took hold of Kosinski's hand and stood up, pulling him with her. "Really, Eddie, this is too much. C'mon, Jerzy, we're getting out of here." She went to get her coat.

"What about the whip?" asked Bunny again.

"Eddie, you are always picking over details like an unsatisfied spinster. I'm not writing true confessions, are you?" Kosinski put on his coat. "Why do you fixate on the vibrator and the whip? As symbols perhaps of some unfinished business?" He smiled warmly and patted her shoulder.

"Perhaps," said Eddie, smiling back, "I had the courage to endure it but you didn't have the courage to write about it."

"Why," ended Kosinski, "are you so sure page 230 refers to you?"

Eddie threw up her hands and imitated Kosinski's accent.

"Woman's intuition," she replied.

Faye returned carrying her coat. "Untie me, Eddie, will you?" She turned her back and presented the thong bow of the phallus.

"You ain't never gonna be no nineteen inches again, Miss

Scarlett, you done had a baby," screamed Bunny in falsetto.
Eddie untied the bow and the phallus clattered to the floor.
Faye gathered it up, stuffed it in her Brearley bookbag, and,
taking Kosinski by the hand, made for the door.

"Don't you want to see my imitation of Kosinski?" shouted
Eddie after her. "I worked on it for months."

"No," said Faye and exited.

"I'd love to see it, Eddie. I'll come by another time." Kosinski followed Faye out the door, shutting it behind him.

Eddie and Bunny laughed. "God, that was heavy," said
Bunny.

"Can you beat it?" said Eddie. "Faye made off with the
prize."

"If I wasn't so wrecked, I would have done the same."
Bunny smiled lewdly. "What about the whip, Eddie?"

Edda shielded her phallus with her hands and struck a mock
pose of innocence. "What about it?" she asked.

"What's it like to be tied down and whipped?"

Edda thought for a moment and then spoke matter-of-factly.

"It's curious," she began. "In bondage, you are forced to
make a mental choice. You can either feel the sensation as
pain, which is simple and immediate, or you can relax completely and investigate it further. If you make enough effort,
you can even turn it into pleasure. It is a parody of the female
experience in concrete physical terms. Going through it was
simply extraordinary. Not sexual. Far more important than that.
I almost cracked. I don't think I could go through it again."

"Hmm," said Bunny. "Interesting. Well, Eddie, what do we
do now? All dressed up and no place to go." She tapped her
phallus. "What time is it—five A.M.—good. I know. We'll
gather up our things and go back to my room at the Stanhope.
We'll bathe in the marble tub, breakfast in the lovely, wood-
paneled dining room, and then go see the latest thing at the
Costume Institute at the Met. We'll do a little shopping at
Bendel's, a new hairdo, perhaps a leg waxing. And in be-

tween, box lunches in Arto's limousine, which I happen to have at my disposal. Don't ask why."

"Oh, how wonderful." Eddie rushed off to change but returned and presented her back to Bunny. "I forgot," she said and Bunny untied the thong bow.

"Bunny," she asked, "why did we put on the phalluses in the first place? Do you remember?"

" 'Cause we thought it was funny."

"Was that all?"

"Yes, no great earth-shattering reason, just that." Edda grabbed her phallus as it fell.

"Oh, Eddie," Bunny exclaimed, "we never read the Alumnae Bulletins. Can I?"

"Of course. Let me go change." Eddie put her phallus into its Brearley bag and took it with her into the bedroom to hide it. Through the door she could hear Bunny laughing as she read of the doings of their former classmates.

Agoraphobia

Marian Root did not like going out in the cold. In truth, she did not like going out at all, but in the hot weather it was easier, and she did go out some, and so people didn't notice.

Marian had read about herself in *The New York Times*. An article in the "Hers" column had convinced her she was an "agoraphobe," a term she preferred to "shut-in" for the visions it conjured up of a white-pillared marketplace in ancient Greece. At first, Marian saw herself in a one-shouldered tunic and one of those braided ponytails, haggling over the price of olives, or gossiping at the wineshop. And then one day it occurred to her that "agoraphobia" meant fear of the marketplace and so, even if she were in ancient Greece, she would never get to the haggling stage. She would be trapped in her own atrium, a prisoner of the same ennui or fear or whatever it was that trapped her now. It depressed her, but still she used the term because it intrigued people.

Marian was between boyfriends and between engagements. By profession, she was a technical proofreader for a number of prestigious medical journals. It was, she was the first to admit, a boring and uncreative job, but it paid well and allowed her to work at home and alone.

By love, Marian was a poet. She had won two poetry prizes in college and later had published poems in several well-known literary magazines. She wanted to apply for a grant to continue her modernization of the couplet form, but she couldn't. That is, she was unable physically to fill out the forms and send them in. They lay, encrusted with soot, atop the last rhymes she had penned about six months earlier. She no longer knew where they were. She had almost forgotten they existed.

It was a slow time of year in the proofreading business, and Marian was on unemployment. Once a week, at 8:30 A.M., she staggered out of her cluttered one-bedroom and somehow made it to the unemployment office. She was always the first to arrive, the first to get her check, and the first to leave, thus ensuring contact with the least number of people. On the way home she stopped at the deli and bought coffee, cat food, and two packs of Vantage Blues. Then she dropped in at the bookstore.

Every Thursday for about two months, Marian had bought herself a self-help book. She had read each one from cover to cover, and was amazed to report that without exception, they were all brilliant. The problems described in each book sounded exactly like hers, and she learned a great deal. She learned so much, in fact, that now she fully understood her own odd behavior. She had a complete grasp of her situation. Her decline was sharply in focus. But although she was able to analyze everything about herself, she was unable to change any of it. She got brighter and brighter and less and less physical. She fantasized herself as a giant head on a spindly, weak little body, as the first woman extraterrestrial on the Upper West Side.

Marian had a rich and fully developed telephone life. It was confronting people in the flesh that troubled her. She did not like the way people's eyes sat in their skulls; it unnerved her. But it was valid to say that although she seldom left her apartment, she actually knew everyone who was anyone and a great deal about them. People could hardly wait to telephone her and tell about their experiences. Because she had read so many books, she knew exactly how to help. Her advice was considered extraordinary. Her cessation of movement went unno-

ticed. Because she possessed so much information about the
goings-on of others, they never suspected she had a problem.

Marian was young and pretty. Due to the smoking, however,
and the lack of sun and sex, she was beginning to get the
brittle look of a leather purse that's been stored too long in the
closet. Her high intelligence had long since ceased to have an
effect on her behavior and she was thin and getting thinner.
"You look like an anorexic Marilyn Monroe," a gay friend told
her when she bumped into him on the way back from unemployment. "Pretty soon there'll be nothing left."

"Forget it, Marian." Dolores was perched on the television,
filing her nails and cracking her gum. "The guy hates women.
One law for you, another for Liza Minnelli. You know how it
works."

Marian was slumped on her sofa, staring at her bookcase,
completely mesmerized by a book spine. *Violations of the
Child Marilyn Monroe*, it read in black spindly type. Violations, violations, the word repeated itself over and over again
in Marian's mind. She had bought the book on a remainder
table for a dollar. She had never read it. It was the title that
got her and continued to get her. And now, perhaps because of
what her gay friend said, it threatened to consume her.
Dolores was having none of it.

"Marian," she said with supreme annoyance, "would you do
something, please? Would you get off your goddam duff and
do one damn thing? Would you go down and get the mail,
Marian? Would you at least do that?" Dolores folded her arms
impatiently and disappeared. Marian went down to get the
mail.

Dolores had been with Marian since she was four. Unlike
most imaginary friends, Dolores had refused to vanish at
adolescence. Instead, she had matured, taking on a corporeal
image not unlike that of a cynical Barbara Eden, or a crusty
and cantankerous Flo. "I'll go when it's time, Marian," she

said, "and that time may be sooner than you think if this bull keeps up. It's boring me to tears."

In the mailbox, Marian found an invitation to Eva and Morgan's Christmas party. "Eva and Morgan," she mused, "Eva and Morgan. It's a big plunge, but if I can do it . . ." She accepted immediately and threw away their unlisted number so she couldn't take it back. Marian had decided to change and nothing was going to stop her.

"I sure am going," she chirped gaily into the telephone receiver. "I wouldn't miss it. Eva says Russell Baker's going to be there."

Harry Henessey gasped with joy. He was only recently out of the closet and was, therefore, inclined to overdo. It was embarrassing for most of his old friends, and too real. They wished he had kept it to himself. His new friends, though, thought there was a star in the night sky when he was born. They called him a "prophet of freedom" and he ate it up. He met them at meetings of a lady psychic named Gretel. She lived up near Saint John the Divine. Together they had seen the light.

"Russell Baker! God, he came once to a Fly Club luncheon. He was adorable and funny. Eva and Morgan are so classy. How do they do it?"

"Money, Harry. They're both loaded." Marian lit a cigarette and felt her bowels tingle from the nicotine. She listened to the wheezing of her chest as Harry chatted on.

"It's so true. You know I've been disinherited, Marian?"

"Only for the moment, Harry. When they get used to the new you, I'm sure—"

"Forget it, Princess, I'm fucked. Blackmail is the only way I'll ever see a penny. Now look: you want to share a cab to Eva and Morgan's? I'm a little nervous going there ever since my metamorphosis."

"Oh, Harry, I'm sorry," Marian began and Dolores shook her head in disgust. Marian was beginning to lie as easily as a publicist. "I can't. I've got another thing first. Forgive me."

"Do you think Heinlein will be there?" asked Harry just before she hung up. She guessed it served her right.

"I don't know, but I hope so. I love seeing my old lovers at parties. It keeps me young. Bye, baby. See you tomorrow."

Marian was having trouble leaving the house. Getting dressed had gone fine. She looked lovely in a black velvet slim skirt, and a powder-blue silk Russian blouse which matched her eyes. Her thick blond hair was clean and, because of the extreme dryness in the air, was standing straight out from her head like Elsa Lanchester's in *Bride of Frankenstein*. Very high heels made her feel slightly dizzy, a combination of the altitude and the unsteadiness of gait. She had on her best jewelry, cold against her skin, and a quilted satin evening coat, also cold to the touch.

Marian was standing with her back to the front door, staring at her television. For a long time now, Marian had felt as if she were connected to the apartment by a circular ion beam that ran through all the electrical machines she owned. She saw it as tunneling from the television through her midsection to the stereo and then around through all the electrical appliances in the room. When she went through the front door, she felt she had to pull out of the connection. She visualized the beam tearing, ripping out of the TV and stereo and dangling from her ribcage. When the door closed behind her, she felt shorted, cut off, juiceless, inert.

Her eyes tacked from the TV to the stereo to the electric typewriter to the lamps to the dustbuster to the telephone. "Of course," she thought to herself as she lifted the receiver and dialed the weather report, "it is merely a hallucination, a hallucination brought on by fear. They spoke about it in the 'Hers' column. Twenty-eight degrees. Wind chill factor of fifteen. Damn. Hell. Damn."

Dolores was nowhere to be found. Marian walked back to

the front door. She opened it, hallucinated a bank of snow in front of her, pushed through it, and closed the door behind her. "I have nothing to lose" was the only thought she allowed in her mind. Her body, however, felt the shock as it was ripped free of its moorings and borne by her intellectual current into the freezing night.

It was so cold that the homeless people were getting frostbite. In emergency rooms all over the city, toes were lost and fingers, tips of noses. The following summer, they would look like lepers. Marian was having trouble getting a cab.

The icy wind raped her as she stood in the street. She wept from the cold. The insides of her nose froze and she couldn't breathe. For a moment, she panicked, and her heart began to knock like an insistent bill collector. Her legs in their flimsy stockings were turning red and her breath glistened in the light of the street lamp. She had a second of high exhilaration, a pure rush of terror, as an empty cab drew up in front of her and stopped. She got in without hesitation. The experience it promised was, quite simply, better than any she now knew.

Marian relaxed in the warmth of the taxi. There was no partition and she was very close to the driver's head. There were photographs of his family on the back of the front seat. A wedding, it looked like, Italian or Greek. She peered over the seat at the driver's license. Something-opolos, Greek. Heinlein had promised to take her to Greece once but he never had. She didn't remember why, so she guessed it wasn't important.

The driver was staring at her now. He looked annoyed. "Where to?" he was asking. "Where you going?"

Marian went blank. She opened her purse and took out a cigarette. She spoke while lighting it. "A party." She chatted nonstop: "God it's cold, I can't think when it was last as cold as this. Hang on just a minute I have the address here somewhere. Women! They're completely *apo-kato*. You know *apo-kato*, right? You're Greek, aren't you?"

The driver beamed. "You speak Greek?" he asked. "You Greek?"

Marian smiled and shook her head no. "Let's see where are we now," she took up chatting again, "West End Avenue."

"Lady—" the driver was losing patience.

"Central Park West. Go over to Central Park West and then we'll discuss it further." Marian sat back and drew on her cigarette. She tried to calm herself. Where was she going? What was Eva and Morgan's address? They had moved into it after college. A prewar apartment with huge rooms. There was a lot of art in it. They collected art. There'd be artists at the party if she ever remembered where it was.

When she and Heinlein were dating, they used to go often to Eva and Morgan's. Eva and Morgan had fun for a living and consequently were slim and trim and very beautiful. They had met in college. They looked alike, and they both loved Yevgeny Yevtushenko. They were among those few who mated for life, who had other things to do besides sampling new lovers. Actually, she didn't get much of a sense of sexuality from them at all. They resembled those ink drawings of young aristocrats from the thirties, and no matter how she looked at them, they weren't very sexy.

Maybe they weren't really happy. Marian didn't know. But once after an all-night party, she had stood with Eva watching the sun rise over the reservoir and Eva had said wistfully—

Marian leaned over the front seat of the taxi. "The reservoir," she said excitedly, "opposite the reservoir on Central Park West. That's Eighty-ninth Street. *Efkaristo.*"

"*Parakalo*," the driver returned, nodding in deference.

Marian fell back against the seat. Her head lolled to one side, and out of the corner of her eye, she watched the pattern of stones on the wall that hems in Central Park. The taxi accelerated and the stones rushed by, hidden only occasionally by some ice-cold hustlers frozen in poses of gimlet-eyed petulance.

She passed the Museum of Natural History and wished she were going there, to the second floor as it had been when she was a child. There was then an entire human nervous system in formaldehyde, and a giant uterus with red light ovaries that lit to show the onset of menstruation. It was a dark and mysterious place, a little frightening perhaps, but correct. Life functions were not taken for granted then. Some belief was needed in them to keep them going, some prayer, some awe.

When the cab stopped at Eighty-ninth Street it came to Marian that she had forgotten to feed the cat. For how long, she did not know. She tried to remember if she had fed the cat that morning, but she couldn't. In her mind she saw Mr. Mewer weeping tears of hunger, convulsing on the kitchen floor, dying of neglect. Her stomach seized up with guilt. A great bubble of anguish rose up the center of her trunk, searing her lungs, and escaped out her mouth in a moan. The cab driver did not turn around. He looked at her in the rearview mirror and said distinctly, "You pay now. Eighty-ninth Street, Central Park West. Three fifty."

Marian nodded but she did nothing. She was completely inert, physically incapable of moving a muscle.

The driver put the cab in neutral and twisted in his seat. "You okay?" he asked. "You sick?"

Marian, who had just discovered the extent of her paralysis and was not yet sure what to do about it, smiled sheepishly and nodded her head. She wanted to explain herself, to talk about some loose ends that had been upsetting her for a while now, this sweater that had only one sleeve left to knit, a ring that had been steadily building in the bathtub, but all that came out of her mouth was, "Agoraphobia."

The driver was intrigued. "Phobos? Agora? Agoraphobos?" he repeated. "I don't get it." He lit a cigarette. "You got the fare?" he asked, suspicious. Marian nodded and flicked her eyes down at her purse and back to him. He reached over the seat, took up her purse and extracted from it a five-dollar bill. "Don't worry," he said, "I make change."

Marian wondered if she'd had a stroke. She wondered if she'd finally gone crazy. She wondered how she would live her life as a quadriplegic, if she could edit with a pencil in her teeth, if it'd be worth it. There was that Irish writer she'd read, who was spastic from birth and whose family pulled him around in a wagon and never suspected he was thinking. How'd he do it? He typed with his toes is how. A triumph of the human spirit is how. A triumph of the human will.

Marian began to sweat. Streams of liquid ran down from her underarms and collected beneath her breasts. She felt as if she were sitting inside a huge wad of cotton candy. Through this dense mist of psychic insulation she could dimly see the canopy of Eva and Morgan's building. She wondered if she could ever reach it, if she could ever push through this filmy, sticky cobweb that surrounded her. She thought not.

Dolores materialized in the front seat, filing her nails and cracking her gum. Her thick blond hair was piled in a beehive on top of her head. Her yellow waitress uniform was crisply starched. It rustled as she moved.

"This is too much, Marian." She took out her gum and stuck it beneath the dashboard. "This is it. This is the last straw."

She twisted in her seat and stared at her motionless friend.

"I remember when you were five, Marian, and the older kids were building a bonfire in the backyard and they wouldn't let you play. You remember what you did? You gathered your own twigs, carried them into the house, and built your own bonfire in the living room. You never took no for an answer, Marian. Your mother could not believe it. Neither could I. We thought you were going to go places. We were wrong."

Marian recalled the incident. She remembered the flames searing the white shag rug. She remembered the power she felt as they leapt up and then the surprise as her mother ran screaming into the living room.

The driver was looking at Marian in the rearview mirror. He was smoking a cigarette and wondering where this fare would end. Every time the meter clicked, he extracted more money from Marian's purse. It was too cold to hassle. He had decided to wait it out.

Dolores was tapping her nails on the leather upholstery. "So, what's it going to be, Marian? Another trip to est? Another mantra? You want to take the Luscher Color Test while we're waiting, or what? I know, let's whip out the tarot cards and see if we can figure out what's going to happen. Uh oh, nine of swords. Sorry, Marian."

Dolores took up her order pad and a small, eraserless pencil. "Let's see, what are you going to have? Eve on a raft of insanity! Sink it! Is that it, Marian, is that what you want?"

Marian shook her head.

"Ever since puberty, you have been a dud, Marian. Where is the child I befriended? Where is that child? You know what your MO is? You get a boyfriend and you come alive. For the six months it lasts, you're like Lynda Carter in *Wonder Woman*, there's nothing you can't do. And when it ends, which it always does, you got nothing left. Suddenly, you're Werner Erhard's wet dream, you know?"

Marian shuddered.

"It's demeaning, Marian, that's the worst thing. And you lied to me, after all these years. You told me we were going to a party, fun and frolic, the whole hog. In truth it's just a one-way ticket to your nervous breakdown. Thanks, Marian. It's been real."

Dolores began to fade. Marian hung her head. "No, please," she whimpered, "don't go."

"Uh-uh, Marian." Dolores was outside the cab, looking in. "No more Miss Nice Guy. You want to spend your thirtieth birthday in Bellevue, go to it. Not this cookie. Angel robes give me the creeps." Dolores had her hands on her hips now. Frost was collecting on her waitress uniform. She was fuming.

"Get out of the fucking cab! Do it, Marian. Do one goddam thing before it's too late. You're not going to sell the Hell's Angels on monogamy, Marian, you're going to a goddam cocktail party. Get out of the cab!"

Marian pushed. She struggled against the opaque substance that enclosed her. She tore at it, clawed at it, elbowed it. She drew from herself the strength of a psychotic and ripped through the film and grasped the handle of the door.

"Open that door, Marian." Dolores was tapping her red high heel on the icy pavement. "Open that door right now or I'll leave you where I found you that first day, sitting in your own shit and whining about it."

Marian nodded. It was true what Dolores said: That first day she had been sitting in her own shit. She had lost control and was sitting on the floor of her room crying, trying to wake her mother up, trying to get her to come fix it. And that was when Dolores made her first appearance.

The driver, aware that she had moved, turned around and held out her purse. Dolores was pacing outside the cab. "I'm sick to death of your tantrums, Marian. I'm disgusted by your laziness, and your dependence on men. I'm revolted by your writer's block and your refusal to get off your ass and clean the house. And I'm appalled—"

"Shut up!" screamed Marian and she pushed down the handle and flung open the door of the cab. She grabbed her purse from the driver and propelled herself, feet first, through the opening and onto the frigid pavement. Behind her, the cab driver pulled the door shut and sped away before she could change her mind.

Marian was out. She was standing on the corner of Eightyninth Street and Central Park West, a few yards from Eva and Morgan's building. "Don't worry, Marian," said Dolores, "you did feed the cat. I saw you do it. He ate a Mixed Grill dinner and some dry food and now he's fast asleep. Enjoy yourself," she added, winking, and vanished.

Marian rushed up the street and threw herself into the gaily decorated lobby of Eva and Morgan's building. She hovered there a moment basking in the warmth of the Christmas-tree lights. Some were those bubbling water candles that light up and make a whirring noise. They seemed to her to be a parody of her own insides. She was exquisitely excited.

She hurried to the elevator, pushed the button, and waited impatiently. She was afraid the fear would get her again. She was afraid she'd lose the energy.

At this moment, a tall man in a Brooks Brothers overcoat entered the building and strode over to the elevator. He pulled off his gloves, blew on his hands to warm them, and then cupped them over his icy cheeks. "Jesus," he muttered.

Marian looked up at him. Her heart skipped and she giggled.

"Excuse me," she asked, "aren't you—"

"Russell Baker." The man nodded and smiled.

She laughed again. The elevator door opened and they got in.

"Oh, Mr. Baker," she blurted as they faced front, "I read your column every Sunday. I just—I love it! Frankly, I don't know what I'd do without *The New York Times*!"

Russell Baker was smiling nervously as the elevator doors closed.

The Lincoln-Pruitt
Anti-Rape Device:

Memoirs of the
Women's Combat Army in Vietnam

Vietnam, Southeast Asia
Latitude 16°18', Longitude 107°29'
February 7, 1968

PHASE I: ILLUSION

As the Chinook took off from Da Nang and banked west
toward the Oma River near LZ My Sinh, Major Lincoln-Pruitt
was putting on lip gloss. For three months her lips had cracked
in excitement and anticipation of this moment, and nothing
had helped until the girl in the PX recommended Yardley's.
Pot o' Gloss, the product was called, and the Major bought a
dozen tiny pots, in the color Ravaged Red just because the
irony appealed to her.

In addition to soothing her burning lips, rubbing the salve
along the contours of her mouth produced in her a tranquiliz-
ing effect, and she began to think of her father and how proud
he would be if he could see her now. In her rucksack she had

his photograph. It was old and battered, but still you could make him out—there, just behind General MacArthur, on the day the Philippines was liberated.

General John Barrymore Lincoln-Pruitt, named, her grandmother told her, for the very handsome movie star who smoked a pipe, had bequeathed to her a strong constitution, a high moral fiber, and a favorite saying. From Proust's *Within a Budding Grove*, it had come to her often in the last three months, precisely at those moments when she felt as if the Operation would never get off the ground, would never be, as it was now, a full-fledged reality. Always, it had given her courage. And so, with the deafening roar of the helicopter blades for cover, in homage to her late father and General Larson back at Fort Dix, and as kind of a pep slogan for the whole Foxy Fire platoon, she uttered it aloud one last time. "Victory," she cried, "belongs to the antagonist who knows how to suffer one quarter of an hour longer."

Captain Zinnia Jackson shifted manically on the metal aircraft seat. Her Leopard, as the platoon fondly called the Lincoln-Pruitt Anti-Rape Device, was pinching again, and try as she might, she could not get comfortable. "Uh-uh," she muttered, shaking her great, bald head and fidgeting, "this is not what I had in mind, no way."

The previous June when she graduated from Smith, Zinnia had applied to the Foreign Service. She pictured herself at an embassy post in Berlin, Beirut or maybe Constantinople, the first black American woman in the high-class spy business. She had been candid at the interview. "I speak six languages fluently. I can hold my liquor. And I have nothing against promiscuity provided it furthers American interests and my career." Better credentials than most, the recruiter had had to agree.

But Zinnia had not been posted to an embassy as she had hoped, she had been passed to the C.I.A., and specifically to the Phoenix Program in Vietnam, to Operation Foxy Fire, the top-secret brainchild of one Major Victoria Lincoln-Pruitt, the highest-ranking female career officer in the United States Army.

"Look, Jackson," the Major had said, "there are no black women F.S.O.s even from Smith. Why the hell should there be? But if you stick by me and do right by my Op, I will personally see to it that you're the first. Bargain?" The Major stuck out her tiny gloved hand.

"Bargain," concluded Zinnia and shook it. And then the Major told her about the L.P.A.R.D., and if her ambition hadn't already clinched the deal, the Leopard would have.

"Let me understand this." Zinnia surveyed the Major with increasing awe. "The L.P.A.R.D. has four instantaneous modes: the Probe, which poisons the human intruder; the Shredder, which pulverizes wooden implements such as broom handles; the Laser, which melts glass bottles and metal bayonets; and an iron cap which descends and makes penetration of any kind impossible. And it runs on—The Major smiled mysteriously.—Microchips."

"And I activate it internally with my pubococcyneal muscles?" Zinnia was amazed at the simplicity. The Major nodded, proud of her invention.

But when Zinnia was issued her weapon, it had proved a bit quirky and tended to pinch. And now, months of training later, en route to her first engagement with the Viet Cong, she made a last-ditch effort to adjust it. With her big brown hands, big-as-a-man's, big-as-a-man's, she yanked up her saffron robe, spread her knees wide, and oiled it once again. Very cautiously, she squeezed her muscles in the drill: *And* Probe—*and* Shred—*And* Melt— *And* FlakCap. Deep inside herself she felt the iron casing descend. And for the first time in her entire life she felt safe even though she wasn't wearing panties.

Corporal Mandy Rasmussen was a white-blond beauty from Hopkins, Minnesota, Raspberry Capital of the World. There were raspberry bushes in her family, passed from generation to generation, and every summer of her life until she was sixteen she picked raspberries and helped her mother sell them at a roadside stand. Whatever berries remained at the end of a day, she would trade to her friends for bootleg Hendrix albums. And it seemed like a good enough gig until the day she dropped acid in the Dairy Queen parking lot and realized she was going nowhere quick.

A casualty of the sixties, as her mother would later describe her, she bolted, and the next thing she knew, she was speeding on the walkway of the I.D.S. building in Minneapolis, and Mr. Bobby Satin was running his fingers through her hair like Havana cigars stirring melted butter. And he was saying, "If I could be of service to you in some small way, it would be like walking in snow on snow."

By the time she and Bobby were arrested in New York City, Mandy was ready to split. "I have been a street hooker for two years," she told the Major in the holding room at the precinct, "and I have seen a lot of things. But I have never seen anything as groovy as the L.P.A.R.D. It turns me on."

So naturally, when the Major offered her the rank of corporal in the Foxy Fire Op, Mandy accepted pronto. "I wouldn't mind killing me a few men," she said with great seriousness. "Men have never done much for me, Mr. Bobby Satin for starters."

But the Major had drafted Bobby too. And now as Mandy watched him hunched over the controls of the Chinook, she could tell that he was scared to death. There was sweat on his neck and he was wearing two flak jackets. She focused on the patches sewn on his back. One spelled out F-O-X-Y F-I-R-E and the other the platoon's motto, MAKE LOVE NOT WAR. The movement of the chopper was making Bobby shake like a junkie doing a cold-turkey trot. And for some reason, the idea of his being afraid made her laugh.

Absentmindedly, Mandy went to play with her hair. It was a

habit of hers since childhood. She would grab a few strands of the white-gold floss, stroke them like a bunny and then sniff them, tripping out on the musty smell, and reveling in some leftover infant self-love. But now her fingers met prickly stubble, and she sighed deeply. She had forgotten. She no longer had any hair, or eyebrows for that matter. Like all the other women in the Foxy Fire platoon she had been shaved as bald as an egg.

"I owe it all to Bob Hope," thought Sergeant Fantasy Smith as she glanced around the Chinook. "If I hadn't been a gypsy in his Christmas U.S.O. show, I wouldn't have been in Saigon and met the Major, and I wouldn't be in combat now. It's all about being in the right place at the right time and don't ever let an agent tell me different."

Her eyes happened to light on Mandy just as she was dragging that weird little bag from her rucksack. A human-hair purse. Just lovely. Mandy had sewn it herself.

After they'd had their heads shaved, Mandy had leapt out of the barber chair and, like a starving monkey in search of lice, picked the tile floor clean of every strand of her waist-length hair. She then fled the building in an animal trot. Later Fantasy found her in the barracks sewing frantically what Mandy described as "a special bag, only for the maintenance tools of the L.P.A.R.D." "Fine, dear." Fantasy was nothing if not tolerant. "Whatever gets you through the night. As long as I don't have to look at it."

And she hadn't. Until now. Now it seemed Mandy had decided to wear it. Right out in the open, no shame, she had attached a thong to it and was putting it on for all the world as if it were a darling Chanel shoulder bag. The matted curls blew in the chopper wind.

Fantasy's eyes fled Mandy and took refuge on the Major, who was oiling her lips. She was reminded of their meeting at a bar in Saigon. "I just got a Dear Joan letter," she had drawled drunkenly at the Major seated on a bar stool next to her. "D'ya ever get one?"

The Major downed her shot of tequila. "Never dated anyone who could write," she said simply.

"Really?" asked Fantasy, impressed.

The Major nodded. "I like men big, strong, and completely illiterate. Talking's the last thing I want to do with a man. They don't make sense."

"Oh you're so right," said Fantasy, spurred on. "My boyfriend's a Marxist. When I left the U.S., he was sitting in at Columbia. Next thing I know, he's gotten married in one of the buildings, probably to a nose-job majoring in art history. Mark Rudd and Tom Hayden were flower boys. He doesn't love me anymore, he says, 'cause I went to Vietnam. I was working, for Christ's sake! The Bob Hope thing is a good intro for a performer. It was that or demonstrating contact lenses at the Coliseum. Which would you choose? He knows I'm apathetic politically. Look, he sends me this."

She unfolded a glossy paper and flattened it on the bar. It was a *Life Magazine* cover showing a young man in a Nehru jacket and a young woman in a granny dress both bestrewn with flowers heading a torchlight parade around the Columbia campus. "That's him." Fantasy ground her finger into the photo. "You know what else?" The Major listened. "I just found out there's only one orgasm. He lied to me." Fantasy slammed her fist on the bar. "I guess I'm the last to know, huh?"

"Look." The Major spoke kindly. "It's not my business, but if you'd like to find yourself, to do your own thing, to get in touch with your existence apart from men . . ."

Fantasy was suspicious. "Does this have anything to do with women's lib?"

"Not exactly," replied the Major.

Two days later, with Mr. Hope's blessing, Fantasy left the tour and returned with the Major to Fort Dix, where she began her training as a junior officer in the Foxy Fire platoon. "Listen," she wrote the girls in the line, "if men can join the French Foreign Legion, why can't I? From now on I shall think of myself as a free-love mercenary. And you know what? When I'm wearing the L.P.A.R.D., I love myself, I really do."

"I do," murmured Fantasy, rearranging the folds of her saffron robe. It was a stunning color, saffron. A cross between ripe peach and sunrise, a perfect complement to her pink-hued skin. She loved the filmy gauziness of the material, the way it fastened at one shoulder, and how nicely the resulting folds caressed her curvy muscles. In fact, except for the sandals, which reminded her of hippies, she adored the entire outfit. She even adored being bald. With the proper eye makeup it was a fabulous look. Luckily, her skull had revealed itself to be the epitome of brachycephaly. No unsightly ridges or scars, just a glowing planetary roundness out of which her blue eyes sparkled like vast oceans on an alien globe.

But it was more than just the aesthetic aspect of the garb that suited her. She felt a deeply spiritual communion with it as well. The outfit, Major Lincoln-Pruitt had explained, the saffron robe, the shaved head and eyebrows, the sandals, was their cover. To the Viet Cong they would appear to be a group of refugee Buddhist nuns drifting across Vietnam wherever the changing tides of war might take them.

The other women didn't understand what a Buddhist nun was. They didn't know Zen or the *I Ching*, and the idea that a rock might have a soul only brought out the sadist in them. But Fantasy was floored. For not two days before she left the States with Bob Hope, a psychic in the Ansonia Hotel had told her: she'd been a Buddhist nun in a previous life.

Master Sergeant Dinah Wentworth hated pimps. In the twenty years she had been a madam, she was proud to say that she had never needed, wanted, or even so much as entertained the idea of having a pimp. "Why on earth," she would ask her girls, "do you work your tails off, day after day, earning money just to give it all away? For what? For the illusion that some-one— Listen—I've been to the war zone. I've worked my way up through the ranks and I'm a general now. I can get down with my warriors, but never that far down." And then, seeing that her words had no effect, she would add with a sigh, "Well, I guess it all depends on whether you're a woof-woof or a thoroughbred."

When Major Lincoln-Pruitt announced that pimps were to be included in the Operation, Dinah was livid. She had marched right into the Major's office and tried, on the spot, to resign. "I have dealt with pimps for twenty years," she thun-dered, "for twenty years I have watched them turn good strong businesswomen into walking tubes of K.Y. jelly and now you . . . you . . ."

"Call me Victoria," Major Lincoln-Pruitt had replied calmly. "I don't like Vicky. It sounds like a cheerleader. Perhaps, had I been called Vicky, I'd be married now with babies. But I didn't want that. Like you, Dinah, I wanted something differ-ent for myself, something stronger, more independent."

"Exactly my point!" Dinah bellowed, pounding the desk. "I have not been pimpless for twenty years to be suddenly sub-mitting—"

The rest of Dinah's sentence turned to mush as the karate-trained palm of the Major's hand smashed into her left cheek-bone and sent her sprawling into the Foxy Fire file cabinet. There was a stunned silence, and then the Major spoke in a childlike tone.

"Don't ever use the word 'submit' in my presence, please, Dinah. Not 'submit,' 'submission,' 'submitting,' or 'submitted.' I don't like the verb or the noun, and, very frankly, the partici-ple does something to me.

"Now. We need the pimps as a support base, Dinah. We need them for transport to and from the landing zones. We need them for fire support should we incur ground attack upon reaching the landing zones. And we will need them for medevac if, for some unforeseen reason, we cannot contain the perimeter by means of the L.P.A.R.D. In that event we will need them very much and very fast, for the Leopard is the only weapon we will have with us."

"I never heard anybody use the words 'pimp' and 'support' in the same sentence before," said Dinah, unconvinced.

"I understand," the Major continued. "And the question is: Why not use our own 101st Cavalry Division, a crack airmobility outfit, to perform these tasks and take us where we want to go? Because Operation Foxy Fire is top secret. Top secret especially from such young men as make up the First Cavalry. And why, Dinah? Because they gossip. They chit-chat over those radios like hens on hormones. And if the Marines get wind of our Op, were they to learn about the Leopard, and, more specifically, how we intend to deploy it, they might find us, well, unorthodox, or worse, challenging. And what is most important to me, more than pimplessness is to you, is that if we do get fucked, it is by the Viet Cong and on our backs."

The Major paused for a moment and then asked apologetically, "You catch my drift now, don't you, Dinah?"

Dinah, who was lying in an awkward position on the floor, tried to pick herself up and nod at the same time. But the pain from her cheekbone made her lose her balance and, once again, she crashed into the file cabinet. Major Lincoln-Pruitt uttered a cry of distress and darted out from behind her desk to give Dinah a hand.

"You won't have a bruise," the Major said proudly. "It's an art I learned long ago. A beating is fine in its place, but a bruise brings a vendetta. Remember that, Dinah, it's true. Want some lip gloss?"

In her life, Dinah Wentworth had respected few men and fewer women, but she worshiped Major Lincoln-Pruitt. For one thing the woman had style. In addition to a well-tailored beige Army tunic and jodhpurs, the Major always wore a highly polished Sam Browne belt, brown pumps with four-inch heels, and skin-tight, chocolate-brown Italian leather gloves that buttoned at the wrist. A beige envelope cap sat jauntily aside her bouffant chestnut hair, and her backbone was ramrod straight, as were her ethics.

She was Radcliffe '51, around thirty-eight years old, four feet eleven inches tall, a confirmed bachelorette and dedicated to the eradication of fear in women. It was for this reason she had invented the L.P.A.R.D., after, she was fond of joking, one too many dates with Harvard men. "Harvard," she would add, "is just another way of saying 'hostile to women,'" and the platoon would laugh. But it became an adjective the women carried with them. Much of the time she reminded Dinah of a highly bred, brilliant and unpredictable Siamese cat. Now she purred. Now in a lightning flash her paw sliced Dinah's cheek. Now she posed behind her desk licking her fur and rubbing on lip gloss.

At last, thought Dinah as she eased herself into the brown leather wing chair opposite the Major's desk, a woman who can go from A to B in a straight line! A woman she could look up to, a woman with a goal. A woman controlled by no human emotion she had ever been subject to—not love, not sex, not money, not fear, not pain, and no, not even anger. Dinah did not know how she knew, but she knew, that it was not out of anger that the Major had cuffed her. No, the action came from some deep-seated, female power instinct that burbled and pumped inside the Major's body in place of the emotion and envy-riddled tissue mass that most women had for hearts. Like a mummy tiger, she had smacked her cub to keep it from danger, and as soon as the act was done, it was gone. And because in her life Dinah had never before sat with another female and felt the absence of female confusion, she began to cry.

The Major, who had just finished pulling on her Italian leather gloves, stretched out her tiny hands, palms up, across the desk. "Button me up please, Dinah," she said, and while Dinah grappled with the doll-size buttons, she made a speech. "Dinah," she began, "I am not a magician. I'm a soldier, a logistics expert, a strategist, a weapons engineer, and a helluva pushover when it comes to men. That's right: a soft touch. The kind of gal who loves Irish Catholic manic-depressive geniuses who can't get it up because they drink too much and drink too much because they can't get it up. The kind of woman who's hypnotized by a smile on the face of a sadist. The point is, I'm like you. I'm like every intelligent woman I've ever known: undermined by my own vulnerability. My hope is that the Foxy Fire Op will change all that."

"Well, how?" Dinah was confused. "How will that change who you're turned on to?"

"The eradication of fear will change everything, Dinah. At the moment I find I am submissive in spite of myself, in a thousand ways I never even suspected. Just when I've plugged up one leak, I spring another one. Too many holes, Dinah. I'm like a Swiss cheese, and a Swiss cheese can't hold water. In other words, every woman is possessed of a mind and a body and no matter what the mind is doing, the body is always vulnerable. This vulnerability eats away at a mind, you know, like rats at—"

"A Swiss cheese?" asked Dinah.

The Major grinned. "And if I don't wish to procreate, if I don't wish to care for a man, if, as is the case, God has given me a superior intelligence and the drive to make it count, if I wish to roam the earth and swashbuckle, must I be stuck with this pulpy biological destiny? This open-mouthed view of the world, waiting to be filled, fearing to be filled, who needs it?"

"Wanting to be filled?" ventured Dinah. "Don't you like sex?"

The Major looked perturbed. "I like sex, Dinah. Of course I like sex. But try and imagine for just a moment a woman for whom sex is only one of the great mysteries and pleasures that

life has to offer, and don't misunderstand. The L.P.A.R.D. is
not an evil device designed to castrate men. It is simply an
intelligent and long-overdue reaction to centuries of Har-
varding."

"Men can be raped but they don't lead their lives fearing it.
Are you sure it's not in the mind?" asked Dinah.

"Do you fear broom-handle rape by other women?" the
Major countered.

"No," replied Dinah.

"Well, then," said the Major, "my point exactly. It's the
others one fears, and I don't like subliminally fearing the opposite half of the human race, Dinah, it interferes with my
existence. And yours. Prostitution is a boring choice, isn't it?"
Dinah said nothing. "When the I.R.S. brought you to my attention, I snapped up you and your girls because I felt, given
the time allotted for training, you were already the best-
equipped group of American women for the sexual type of
combat dictated by the L.P.A.R.D. It spared me having to deal
with guilt, at least. But I'd rather have cheerleaders, if the
truth be told, for a true control, women without an attitude.
Well, I have Smith and Jackson, and myself. We'll see how we
fare in the field. Thank you."

The right button of the Major's glove finally slipped through
the buttonhole. She stood up, walked around her desk, past the
file cabinet, past Dinah in the wing chair, over to the picture
window that fronted on the Fort Dix parade ground. Outside
the Foxy Fire platoon was doing Tai Chi: infinitesimal preci-
sion movements that from the Major's vantage point made
them look like a crowd of Madame Alexander stop-action
puppets. She peered intently at them as she went on.

"On the other hand, Dinah, the prostitutes in the platoon
have, in a sense, dealt directly with the questions I am raising.
The answer you have come up with, as I see it, allowing yourself to be constantly violated but getting paid for it, seems to
me only an anesthetic and definitely not a cure. Which brings

me back to pimps. We need them to drive the choppers, not our women. So, Dinah, I'm leaving it to you to prevent all fraternization. Remember: Repressed sexual energy is the stuff of which heroines will be made. I trust that's clear. You are dismissed."

It was quite clear, and Dinah had carried out her orders and then some. The women of the Foxy Fire platoon were in a state of pure, aggressive sexual desire, brought on partly by their long isolation from men, and partly by the tiny amounts of Spanish fly which Dinah slipped into the food of everyone including herself but excepting the Major. The effect was hardly noticeable, really. The women were a bit short with each other, "bitchy," men might call it. Their bodies were languid and hot, and chemicals shot into their loins and out again, causing a confusing but delicious agony. "Combat-ready," Dinah reported at the final briefing in Da Nang.

Only once before had Dinah felt so patriotic, and that was when she had left the grim Welsh mining town of her birth to come to America for good. It was fifteen years since that other moment in time when, encased in the furry roar of a flying machine, she had awoken to a purple-caked sunrise over the grid pattern of New York City. She had to her name a fifty-pound note and a newfound friend in the person of a G.M. salesman who occupied the seat next to her. And, of course, that feeling, that glory surge in the pit of her stomach that she felt again now.

Maybe it was the vibration of the Chinook that brought it back to her. Or maybe knowing that she was about to be involved in a moment of history. Or maybe it was just the Spanish fly. But the pimp crew doing rear guard in the chopper, Count Flash Flash, The Jockey, and Vain Johnson, suddenly looked almost attractive. Sitting side by side on their helmets, their bodies hunched over like three great bears on chamberpots, they looked almost desirable, almost cute. And that stabbing intensity which she had so lately defined as patriotism, suddenly metamorphosed into an unfamiliar glee. "My God, it's been years since I actually wanted to have sex," she thought to herself, amused. "I think I'm going to enjoy this war. I'm ready for any major thrust the enemy can deliver." And she laughed. And then for no reason at all, she was reminded of her girlhood in Wales, when, of an afternoon, she would traverse the neighborhood, isolating the younger children from the herd, and reading aloud to them from the newspaper the gory details of malicious sex crimes.

The Chinook was beginning its descent. A sudden jerk as the chopper dipped and hovered over LZ My Sinh snapped Major Lincoln-Pruitt to attention. Her eyes whipped toward the cockpit and collided with those of Bobby Satin and his copilot, Mr. Snow, who had instinctively turned to look at her. Six eyelashes flapped in the appointed wink, and she nodded and stood up.

Over the whine and thunder of the engines, the Major screamed with a delicious thrill her first combat order—"Pimps Up"—and stood by as the Count, the Jockey, and Vain Johnson snatched at their M16 rifles, grabbed for their helmets, and stumbled crazily toward the open door. They were driven, she noted with amusement, by fear and its bullying intimate adrenaline. The absence of courage or sense of purpose in their mission gave them all the dignity of three winos on fire. "Men," she thought to herself, "typical men ruled by terror, ego, and testicle—like dogs, like silly dogs with high-heeled feet who alternately cower and bark and always end up running in circles." No wonder they couldn't win this war. This was a war of stealth, and stealth was the province of women and cats, as the Foxy Fire Op would soon prove.

The women of the platoon were ready. Like a field of wigless Barbie dolls, they swayed from side to side in the wind of the landing chopper, their faces upturned and basking in the visionary light that emanated from their leader. The Major was

ready too. On tiptoes now, her saffron robes swirling frantically, her tiny hands cupped around her glossy mouth, her
pointy skull glistening, her eyes tightly closed, in a super-
human baby effort, she called out to them. Like a mad little
bird in the grip of a hurricane, she screeched, "Retract position
FlakCap!" The women did so. "And Probe!" she screeched
again, and this too was done. And the only evidence of action
was a mass guttural sigh as twenty hairless females concentrated on their innermost female workings. There was no ex-
ternal movement, no visible change to signal it, but the three
pimps cringing nearby trembled in disgust at the sight. Only
they, and the Joint Chiefs of Staff, knew the power of the
occurrence. Once a bevy of luscious breasts and thighs, in a
trice the platoon of women had become: a cache of human
punji sticks.

The chopper was hovering at ground level. The three pimps
leapt out and deployed themselves around the LZ, searching
for enemy contact. For a moment, the high scream of the
chopper blades and the grim roar of the engine created a sense
of battle panic. Spasmodically, the pimps ran to and fro across
the forest clearing, clutching the M16s like new Christmas toys
they had vowed never to share. The noon sun glinted off the
patches on their flak jackets. As they darted around the LZ, the
words MAKE LOVE NOT WAR seemed to clang off their backs and
hang in the humid air like the afterglow of popping flashbulbs.
When, to no effect, they had menaced the surrounding forest
in a 360-degree perimeter, they returned to the chopper door
and awaited further orders.

The women had gathered their belongings and were ready
to disembark in twos. The Major was the first to go, but before
she did, she smiled broadly at the women in her command and
raised her tiny fingers in a V for victory. As she was plunging
onto the grass below, she was heard to chirp, "Okay girls, let's
get some!"

Two by two, the women filed out of the chopper. They

extended their slender arms and hands to the pimps waiting tensely on the ground, and, in a series of gazellelike jetés, sailed gracefully onto the LZ.

When they were all safely accounted for, the pimps unloaded the supplies. Four boxes of dried astronaut food, enough protein for weeks, and guaranteed to keep the weight down; twelve battery-driven chain saws and The Army Hootch-Building Manual; one box of gaily-colored prayer strips, Buddha posters, votive candles, and other equipment for the Buddhist shrines; one box of seeds, hoes, and fertilizer for the kitchen gardens; six boxes of party items for use in conjunction with the L.P.A.R.D.; twenty tape recorders with selected tapes, twenty mirrors, forty hits of Sunshine, a case of champagne, a gross of massage oil, twenty lava lamps, two cartons of body paint, twenty bottles of Chanel No. 5, one stack of girlie magazines, and two dozen cans of smoked oysters. Last to be unloaded were the pagoda, the rugs, twenty pink plastic raincoats, a wheelbarrow, and one large carton of Army-issue body bags.

The three pimps headed for the Chinook. Those who had been their women before the Foxy Fire Op began, rushed to kiss and hug them goodbye. The pimps glanced at Sergeant Wentworth and fled in terror through the chopper door. Wentworth laughed. The women waved mournfully, and the big Chinook began to ascend. "Be back on the fifteenth unless otherwise ordered," the Major shouted to Bobby Satin. "We'll be here with our body bags," she added cheerfully, "or on them."

The big Chinook rose into the sky. Count Flash Flash, the Jockey, and Vain Johnson huddled around the cockpit, and, with Bobby Satin and Mr. Snow, stared at the scene receding below.

"Three months without pussy," muttered Bobby Satin. "Three no-fucking months."

"Hey man," said Mr. Snow, always the voice of reason, "it was blue balls or a two-year tour in 'Nam, right up front within kissin' distance of the gooks. No pussy for a year beats that shit."

"Dig it," said the Jockey. "You saw those slides Wentworth showed us: Venus Jackson, the number-one player in Cleveland, three Eldorados in three colors with lizard seats—drafted, man, by mistake. No arms, no legs—they call him V. A. Venus now. He ain't never gonna get no pussy again."

"I'm a lot smarter since I ain't gettin' any," said Vain.

The pimps were silent for a while, and then Bobby murmured sadly, "I have lost my bottom woman. Mandy ain't gonna be good for shit after this."

"Yeah, man," said the Jockey plaintively. "But I got to pity those unsuspecting gooks. I mean, I have tried to imagine . . ." The Jockey, reminded of his testicles, took his helmet off his head and sat on it instead. The Count and Vain quickly followed his example.

"Indeed, brother," said the Count, "they gonna get laid to rest."

"Poor motherfuckers," said the Jockey. "You think they go quick?"

"Not quick enough," said Bobby.

"It's times like this I thank God that I'm an American," the Count began, but was interrupted by a storm of static emanating from the chopper radio.

"This is the 101st Cavalry, Chopper 92467. Identify yourselves, please. Over."

An all-American whitebread voice boomed out of the speaker, and the five pimps looked at each other in fear. Just over the horizon, Bobby Satin could see the Cobra gunship approaching. It was speeding toward them now, a giant black mosquito intent on sucking blood. Bobby got on the radio.

"This is Chopper 1, Foxy Fire Op. Returning to base. Over."

Inside the Cobra cockpit, Captain Tom Davis and First

Lieutenant Larry Hayes were smoking dope and listening to a tape of The Dead at the Avalon Ballroom. Garcia was just finishing a great riff in "Dark Star" as the big Chinook came into view.

Hayes and Davis were not supposed to be flying, but as 1st Cav officers on their second tours, they did as they goddam pleased. Often of an afternoon they would take up the gunship to survey the countryside, get stoned, listen to tapes, or what-have-you. What-have-you often included strafing Vietnamese villages, annoying Marines on patrol, or, as was the case today, attaching a dragon kite to the gunship's tail and flying between the wind currents to keep it aloft.

"Foxy Fire Op?" said Davis. "What the hell is that?"

"I don't know, Tom," said Hayes, "but I'd hate myself in the morning if I didn't find out." Hayes dipped the gunship and sped by the Chinook cockpit as close as he could go. The big dragon kite danced on the wind currents as Bobby and the others watched in amazement.

Davis and Hayes took a good look. "Well," said Davis, laughing, "it's five black dudes in ten flak jackets with big shiny patches. I'd like to get me one of those. What did they say?"

"MAKE LOVE NOT WAR, Tommy," Hayes replied.

"How interesting," said Davis, banking low now so as to make the dragon snap.

"Uhhuh," agreed Hayes as they passed the Chinook and Garcia segued into "Wharf Rat," causing goose bumps to rise on his neck, "Uh-huh, and how I'd like to."

After a short reconnaissance patrol into the forest, Major Lincoln-Pruitt had decided that LZ My Sinh itself was the perfect spot to set up operations. The Oma River lay about six miles eastward through the forest. And if her calculations were correct, about a mile and a half to the west lay the Viet Cong hamlet stronghold of An Hui.

Deploying themselves on the LZ would not only save the

women the back-breaking work of clearing another site, it would make it easier for them to leave when the time came—especially when one considered the dead weight of the body bags they'd be lugging with them. As for the lack of cover, well, that was the beauty of the Foxy Fire Op: The less cover the better. As the Major had pointed out at the final briefing in Da Nang, "Visibility, vulnerability, and accessibility are the names of the game in this woman's war. The success of this operation depends, oddly enough, as does the Miss America Pageant, on poise, a neat appearance, and your ability to look adorable under pressure."

And so, right on the LZ where they landed, the women of the Foxy Fire platoon began to build their camp. Shelter being the first priority, Sergeant Fantasy Smith and Corporal Mandy Rasmussen took up their chain saws and, with ten other women for escort, meandered over to the treeline to cut wood.

Le Van Dong was the leader of the National Liberation Front cadre in the hamlet of An Hui. Today was his birthday. He was twenty-three years old. He was taller than most Vietnamese, a strapping five feet nine, and it was said in the hamlet that his ancestors must have smiled most favorably upon his birth. For despite the fact that he had spent twenty of his twenty-three years torn by the fortunes of a ruinous and soul-destroying war, he had survived completely unscathed.

His face was unlined, a masterpiece of delicately chiseled features. Cradled in their midst lay two glistening sable-brown slope eyes which, like an LZ, seemed to peep openly and good-naturedly through the densely tangled jungle vines that were his eyelashes.

As he stole through the forest in his black pajamas, his AK-47 Kalashnikov rifle slung over one shoulder, a dead wild pig for supper over the other, he thought to himself that there was only one thing he regretted about fighting this war. He was still a virgin.

As he moved across Vietnam, organizing hamlet after hamlet, teaching the tenets of Ho Chi Minh, laying the foundation for the people's government that would someday rule his land, he had never found time to have a woman. Oh, there were hamlet girls he could have had, plenty of them longing for solace and comfort from the war, who saw in him a security and strength they would dearly love to have tasted. But that was the problem. They were part of the old structure. What they wanted was husbands and children, rice paddies and gardens, water buffalo and, above all, newly built ancestral shrines on which to base everything, to give it meaning in perpetuity, to soften the concept of death. Because he could not give these things, he had withheld himself. It would have been cruel to exploit them.

The women in the cadres, well, they were fine for comrades. But they were so embittered by the war, so desensitized and hard, that they no longer seemed able to make human contact. Though he did not blame them for it, they simply failed to bring out the longing in him.

"Le!" The voice of Ao Dai hissed through the silence of the forest and he stopped in his tracks and waited for her appearance.

The overhead sun in its persistence was shooting downward through the trees, great shafts of light, which here and there pierced the darkness of the forest and created, as they reached earth, a random series of spotlit areas. Here a startled lizard. There a dozing bird. Here the mottled upturned leaves of a sun-starved vine. There the grim little figure of Ao Dai. Like a small dark thundercloud, she traversed the light shafts, hugging her stolen M16 rifle to her breast, her ragged black pajamas stained with sweat, her tiny black pigtails stiff in the current of her personal wake.

"Le," she hissed again, "something has happened. Come!" And he followed as she ran furtively in the direction of the forest clearing known as LZ My Sinh.

•   •

Tran Van Luc, head of the hamlet Cult Committee, stood with some of the elders just beyond the treeline. Ho Chi Minh, namesake of the great leader and second-in-command of the cadre, was there too, as was Tu Do, the hamlet drunk. The men were so transfixed by the scene that was unfolding on the LZ, that they hardly noticed as Le and Ao Dai came among them.

"What is it?" whispered Le. "What's happened?" The squat, round figure of Tu Do did a drunken jig amidst the leaves, and, with a leering grin, pointed toward the clearing. "Well, if you ask me," he said excitedly, "the ancestors have come through."

Le brushed aside the leafy branch that blocked his view and peered onto the LZ. What filled his field of vision was a woman, that much was sure, a non-Vietnamese woman of good health and fair skin. Her head was shaven, as were her eyebrows, and she wore robes of saffron. At first glance, he was reminded of his distant childhood, of early mornings when his house tinkled with the wind chimes of his mother's laughter— the result, she would confide in him mischievously, of her having turned away yet another Buddhist nun on a mission of conversion. Was this woman a Buddhist nun? He focused on her again.

In her hand she carried a saw, which now she placed at her feet. Another woman joined the first now, also bald and in saffron robes, but otherwise quite different. This one was smaller, for one thing, with delicate birdlike bones, tiny hands and feet, and skin as white as the sand on the shores of the South China Sea. The blue of her eyes matched the blue of the sky in such a way as to make Le physically uneasy. He shifted his position behind the trees, looked away for a moment, and then looked back.

Now she too was placing the saw she carried on the ground. As she did so, he noticed a little bag around her shoulder. A bag fashioned from the long-haired, honey-colored fur of some unknown animal. There were buttons on it too. Most bore European writing that he could not read, but one he recognized immediately. He had seen it on some Marines and in news pictures from America. It was a white pictograph on a black background, and, to the Americans, it symbolized peace.

She rose from the ground, and he noted with satisfaction that she wore sandals like his—made from the discarded tire treads of passing transport trucks. And then, his eyes fastened on something that almost made his heart stop: Around her mouselike ankle a chain of gold sparkled in the sunlight. Five golden European letters nestled in the district of her anklebone, perhaps, he hoped, spelling out her name. Determinedly, he concentrated on the letters and tried to remember back to his few short years at the French school. "Em," he murmured softly, "Ah, En, De, Y-grec. Mandeh. Mandeh." He pronounced it again with uncharacteristic gentleness. "*Elle s'appelle Mandeh.*"

Sergeant Fantasy Smith and Corporal Mandy Rasmussen set down their saws at the treeline and began to converse.

"Are you scared?" Fantasy was asking as she glanced slowly around the LZ.

"Of what?" Mandy's tone was derisive. "Of the unknown men who might come in the night? Don't make me laugh."

"Yeah, well, what if the unknown men come in the night firing their machine guns first and using come-on lines later? Still laughing?"

"I've had weirdos," said Mandy, nonchalantly rummaging through her human-hair purse. She extracted a fat brown bottle of suntan oil. "Here. This stuff's great. I used this when Bobby took me to Orlando on vacation. I never looked better. We came back to town and I was the hit of Eighth Avenue. Every guy who came in the place picked me. I made three-fifty a night till my tan faded. Want some?"

Fantasy nodded. "Yeah, it's true. I wouldn't mind being

shot. It's violent and vicious sexual abuse and mutilation I fear. Or did. Why do you think so many men rape and kill women?"

"Because they can," said Mandy matter-of-factly.

"Well, supposing vast numbers of civilian women had the L.P.A.R.D., do you think as many women would be seducing and killing men?"

"I guess."

"I don't. I don't think women are that interested in physical displays of power. Take down your top so I can do your back, and then you do mine."

Mandy and Fantasy fiddled with their saffron robes until in one simultaneous drop, the gauzy material fell from their shoulders and descended around their hips. Behind the treeline, there were two short gasps as Ho Chi Minh and Le Van Dong were presented, for the first time in their lives, with the very close-up sight of four perfect Caucasian breasts crowned with four red-rose nipples which, now that they were exposed, proceeded almost defiantly to stiffen in the breeze.

Ho Chi Minh and Le Van Dong turned away in embarrassment and looked at each other in confusion. "What should we do?" Ho asked Le.

Le replied curtly, "Watch and wait."

"At last," said Tu Do, who was standing nearby, "good advice from the Communists."

Le and Ho brushed aside the leaves again just as Mandy's birdlike fingers, wet with oil, bumped over Fantasy's collar bone. "Oh, that feels good," Fantasy moaned softly. "Ohh."

"If there's one thing I can do it's give a massage," said Mandy. "Bobby wants me to get my license so I'll have something to do when I retire. But don't bet on it. Oh God, doing this is turning me on. God, I need some sex."

"Me too." Fantasy was concentrating intently as she rubbed, lest her fingernails accidentally make scratches on Mandy's snow-white skin.

"I don't know," continued Fantasy. "On the other hand, there are some guys I wouldn't mind offing just for the fun of it. A brooding stage manager I dated when I was doing *Two for the Seesaw* in stock, to name but one. You think it's the Leopard making us sexy?"

Mandy was massaging oil into Fantasy's back. "Maybe. If power turns you on."

Fantasy pondered this. "You know *Two for the Seesaw*? You ever see it?"

Mandy shook her head.

"Well, it's about this really nice bohemian girl who lives in Greenwich Village and men are always using her. And she has an ulcer and a sense of humor, maybe because of it, we're not sure. Anyway, she meets this nice married guy—Robert Mitchum in the movie, God, Robert Mitchum—and they have an affair and teach each other something."

"So?" asked Mandy, turning so Fantasy could do her back.

"So she's a great person but a doormat for men. I think we're doing this for her."

Mandy looked blank. "I thought we were doing this for Nixon and Westmoreland."

"I'm talking about the more cosmic implications. Damn, I wish I could remember her name. But the point is, she was into free love before her time and everyone put her down for it," Fantasy persisted. "But she herself was pure. Fifties morality. Don't you identify with her a little bit?"

"No," replied Mandy and screwed the top on the suntan oil.

"C'mon, you girls, let's get movin'!" The booming voice of Captain Zinnia Jackson pushed away the awkward moment. Mandy and Fantasy watched the giant Negress striding toward them. "The sun be goin' down soon enough and where you broads goin' to sleep? In the trees? There be tigers here, babies. Let's get goin' with that wood."

· ·

Tran Van Luc, head of the Cult Committee, was considered a scholar. Although he could not read and write, he was, in fact, an eminent oral historian, and the repository for a great deal of gossip and information that filtered its way back and forth across Southeast Asia.

He was an expert on the origin of things, especially Man. Often in the evenings he would gather together the children, and regale them with stories of how the races came to be. How the African got his skin was his particular favorite. Over the years, he had embellished it, putting special emphasis on burning desert suns, ancestry of the great apes, and primeval mud baths, all in an effort to explain what was, to him, an amazing earthly occurrence.

Once, in a master stroke, he had told the children that in the beginning, when the ancestors got together to make the first map of the world, a quarrel had erupted over which ancestors would be responsible for which men. The Great Mapmaker strove to pacify them, inking and reinking lines of demarcation on the vast graph paper of the sky. But the ancestors came to blows. As they struggled, the inkpot of the Great Mapmaker tipped over, and a rain of black ink cascaded from the heavens and splashed on the continent of Africa, which lay directly below. And the people of that land, who stood together awaiting the outcome of the quarrel, were covered in jet-black ink. Only the animals, who ran for cover when the inkrain began, escaped unstained. And many of them possess, to this day, black spots and stripes which serve no purpose but to stand in testimony to this sorry event.

"And that, dear children," he would say, "is why they call it 'the Black Continent.' "

"And are the people really black?" the children would ask.

"Indeed. They look like us but they are black as ink," he always replied with great certainty.

But the truth of the matter was that until he saw Zinnia Jackson, her huge feet planted not five yards from where he was hidden among the leaves, he had never seen a Negro in his life.

"Tigers," said Mandy as she and Fantasy retrieved their chain saws from the grass. "What are you talking about tigers, Zinnia? There's tigers here?"

Zinnia nodded solemnly. "Sure is. I've got a cousin on River Patrol, writes to my aunt. He sees tigers three, four times a week."

"Gee, I'd like a tiger coat," said Fantasy wistfully. She scanned the treeline just in case.

"Just forget it, baby," said Zinnia. "We ain't got guns. And 'less we got guns, we can't get tigers."

Zinnia rested for a moment in the sun, the chain saw balancing on her massive shoulder.

"Zinnia," asked Fantasy, "why are you doing this?"

"It's just a rung on the ladder," Zinnia replied. "Something I had to do to get closer to the top. It's just a job to me."

"A Smith grad forced to screw her way to success—nice," laughed Mandy.

"Anything's better than typing," said Zinnia.

"Okay, but how do you feel about the L.P.A.R.D.?" asked Fantasy.

"Well," Zinnia measured her reply, "I feel . . . impregnable. I feel like a female fortress. I feel . . . free."

"Why?" Mandy was perplexed by this outburst.

Zinnia did an impromptu jig. "Because no one can rape me, girl. It's like a dream come true. I am a big, strong woman, Mandy, bigger and stronger than many men. But a midget with a gun and an erection could pull me, until the Leopard came along."

"Hmm. I don't care about rape. I never think about rape," said Mandy. "I only think how exciting it's going to be to seduce a man and then kill him. To expose sexual coupling for the theater of war it truly is."

The other women looked dismayed.

"What? We're not allowed to say it? That's what we're doing. Our submissiveness is only an illusion, that's what the Major says."

Zinnia stared at the forest before her. "Let's pray she's right, babies," she said.

Tran Van Luc edged closer to the treeline. Carefully, he parted the overlapping leaves, but the inkwoman was so tall all he could glimpse was her enormous torso. She wore, as did the others, the saffron robes of the Buddhists. But surely, he thought, were there some special sect of white and ink women, he would have heard of it—in a song, a legend, or as a passing reference in some obscure koan. But then again, he thought sadly, perhaps not. Perhaps there were many wondrous events and wisps of human knowledge that had never and would never filter across the earth and, through him, enlighten the ignorance of An Hui. If nothing else, the war had taught him that.

But, he argued, transfixed by Zinnia's chest, he sincerely had no idea that female breasts could be so large. Were he to write a poem about them, there was simply no fruit he could compare them to. Even with poetic license—no melon, no nut, no vegetable. "Ah, there. You see," he said to himself. "In Africa there must be giant things, growing all over, and I never even suspected."

He knelt down, parted the leaves again, and looked up at Zinnia's face. Huge wide cheekbones and the kind, brown eyes of the water buffalo. Her nose was flat against her face, and her lips were as lush and pink as, ah, as an overripe Chinese pomegranate—yes, that was apt. Sweat poured from the corners of her eyes and dropped like tears onto her pendulous earlobes. In fact, there was sweat all over her, glinting in the sun, and causing the saffron cloth to cling to her body between her breasts and thighs. Into a belt around her waist were sewn round little mirrors which reflected the leaves behind which he was hidden. Talismans, he supposed. He searched for some sign in the mirrors, but his view was blocked by Zinnia's mountainous hand, wiping the sweat off itself. Her hand, he thought, could throw a human head as easily as I have thrown the yarrow stalk to consult the oracle.

"Well," said Zinnia, selecting a branch, "let's get to it." Mandy and Fantasy picked up their saws and made ready, as did the other women of the platoon, who stood poised, waiting for the signal all along the treeline. Zinnia positioned her saw. "I'm gonna take me some frustration out on these trees. I ain't been laid in over three months, babies. First my Leopard hurt so much, I didn't care. But now . . ."

Zinnia switched on her saw, and a thunderous whine shattered the surrounding air. Mandy, Fantasy, and the others did likewise, and the cacophony that resulted was worse than any artillery barrage Le had ever witnessed. He grabbed his ears in agony, and, with Ho Chi Minh and Tran Van Luc, fled back from the treeline. Through the leaves, the women could be seen, their bodies shaking at high speed, their breasts and thighs bobbling wildly, their bald heads bent to their appointed task.

Like the raucous laughter of a frat house of harpies, the scream of thirteen chain saws serrated Ao Dai's skull. She shouldered her M16 rifle and trained it on Mandy Rasmussen. The white woman's head was stuttering in and out of the sight, but Ao Dai waited. And when she had accustomed herself to the staccato dance, when she was sure of the timing, she began to pull the trigger.

"No!" With all the strength that had ever been aroused in his sinewy forearms and chest, Le seized upon the object closest to his grasp and hurled it at the taut figure of Ao Dai. Sixty pounds of dangling pig bone and bloody muscle flew grotesquely through the shadows and, with the deadly accuracy of an Argentine bolo, careened onto Ao Dai's neck and tried to strangle it.

In a frenzy of outrage and horror, she crashed to the forest floor. A random spot of sunlight showcased her fury as, wildly and psychotically, she clawed at the furry dead thing that now all but smothered her face. Ho Chi Minh ran for her fallen rifle and stood by with it. Le Van Dong and Tran Van Luc each grabbed a sticky pig's foot and dragged the matted carcass off her.

"No!" said Le Van Dong.

"No!" said Tran Van Luc.

"No!" said Ho Chi Minh.

Ao Dai sat up and, like a mad little cat who has fallen in water, sputtered and shook herself, her arms and hands flailing crazily.

"They are the enemy!" she wailed, pawing at the pig's blood that was caking on her neck. "They will kill us!"

"We don't know that," said Le without emotion.

"No," said Ho Chi Minh.

"No," said Tran Van Luc, "we don't know that."

"I know it!" Ao Dai screamed, pounding the forest floor. "I know it! They came by American helicopter. They came to kill us!"

"By American helicopter?" said Le almost to himself. "Did you see it?"

"No," rasped Ao Dai, "but I heard it and I know."

"I heard it too and I don't know," began Tran Van Luc.

"They are dressed as Buddhist nuns," said Ho Chi Minh.

"They have made no secret of their arrival," added Tran.

"Yes, they want us to know they are here," agreed Le.

"It is wrong to kill something you don't understand." Tran Van Luc turned back toward the LZ.

"It is wrong to kill something that might be innocent." Ho Chi Minh searched the leaves once again for Fantasy.

"They have no guns," said Le, closing the subject.

"It's a trick," cried Ao Dai, leaping to her feet. "It's a shameful, imperialist trick. These women are American aggressors—tigers dressed as water buffalo. They have no guns that we can see, but mark my words."

The three men were no longer listening. They had drifted slowly away and were standing once more, their hands shielding their ears against the whine of the saws, mesmerized by the quivering women just beyond the treeline. Ao Dai stared after them a moment in disgust. Then she kicked the broken body of the pig at her feet and, like a bad fairy, she crept away muttering prophecies, into the forest.

About a hundred yards down the LZ, Major Lincoln-Pruitt and Sergeant Dinah Wentworth were discussing logistics.

"Our hamlet"—the Major, as she spoke, was drawing on a box of dried astronaut food—"will be built on the simple, circular pattern of most primitive settlements, with the curious Vietnamese exception that there are to be no structures facing either west or northwest."

"Why?" asked Dinah.

"Because of the Five Demons, Dinah. The Five Demons whose wrath we cannot afford to incur at this moment in time, I'm sure you'll agree. Now. At the center of our semicircle is the traditional 'hearth area,' in which we will place the crowning glory of our cover, the bait, the Trojan horse—a structure brilliantly executed by a gay friend of mine who does props for the Met, the prefab pagoda. Do we have the pagoda?"

Dinah rummaged through one of the cartons and found it. "We have the pagoda."

"Good. Now, the pagoda in An Hui is, of course, dedicated to the tiger. But I think it's only proper that ours should be dedicated to the L.P.A.R.D., or Leopard, and, thereby, totemically speaking, to the success of the Foxy Fire Op."

"Lovely," said Dinah. "Of course."

"All right." The Major continued, "Beyond that, there will be
two special differences between most primitive settlements and
our own: the absence of any barrier hedge or wall surrounding
our hamlet; and the presence, in each of the living huts, of two
doorways—one facing the forest and one facing the hearth
area. In this way, each woman or her silhouette will, at all
times, be visible, or, if you will, on display, to anyone standing
at the edge or just behind the treeline."

"Reminds me of Amsterdam," said Dinah wistfully.

"Exactly!" The Major smiled. "Outside of each hut, facing
the forest, each woman will plant and keep her own kitchen
garden. Fruit trees, potatoes, and corn."

"Why?" Dinah did not have a green thumb and was not glad
to hear this. "We'll only be here for a short time."

"Two reasons, Dinah. One: to keep busy while awaiting
contact. And two: for the women of An Hui, for after. Without
the men, there'll be a food shortage until they reorganize.
Think of it as an offering, the least one woman can do for
another, something to make up for . . . war. We have good,
strong, American seeds, the best fertilizer. The gardens will
have a high yield. You never take something, Dinah, without
giving something in return. It's a basic female principle and
one with which, in your line of work, you are more than
familiar."

"True enough," said Dinah. "Go on."

"Yes. Now. Each hut will have its own altar to the Spirit of
the Soil, and whatever other deities and ancestors each woman
cares to propitiate. It's up to the individual."

"The Spirit of the Soil?" Dinah was incredulous. "What
Spirit of the Soil?"

"The Vietnamese Spirit of the Soil without whom you cannot
even think of placing wood on earth."

"Major, you don't really believe . . ."

"I believe in everything, Dinah, especially when I'm in Asia
and at war. The huge, splayed foot of the American Marine

has trampled more than one sacred ground in this part of the world—don't take it lightly, Dinah." The Major shook her head. "Fools! Those fools! Damn right the male mind is better at math. What is sad is that they're proud of it."

The Major paused for a moment and stared at the treeline. "All right." She checked her list. "Where were we? Kitchen gardens. Individual hut allowances. Ready for supply check, Dinah?"

"Ready."

"Okay. Each hut will be issued: one flokati rug."

"Twenty flokatis, check."

"One battery-operated, red-colored, lava lamp."

"Twenty lamps, check."

"One Sony tape recorder and the following four cassettes: 'Sinatra's Hits'; 'The Doors—The End'; 'The Who Sell Out'; and 'The Soundtrack from *Breakfast at Tiffany's.*' "

"Twenty recorders and eighty cassettes, check. Gosh, I adore 'Moon River,' " Dinah sighed in a Welsh accent. "It was my theme song for years. Can I put it on?"

"An equipment check?" said the Major. "Why not? Do you think we can hear it, over the saws?"

Happily, Dinah unwrapped a new cassette and popped it into one of the recorders. She fiddled a moment, fast-forwarding and rewinding, and when it was just where she wanted it, turned up the volume full-strength, and pushed ON.

Like a smooth light show at an acid-rock concert, the voice of Johnny Mercer swelled and nestled itself between the whines of the chain saws. And all along the treeline, the women of the Foxy Fire platoon began to waltz to the music of Henry Mancini. Leading their chain saws like the men of their dreams, they twirled in and out of the trees, accenting the cadence of the downbeat, with the raspy, searing roar of their machines.

It became a new-wave symphony. John Cage would have creamed. Bob Fosse would have died. John Simon would have called it "pretentiously intellectual." But it was just one of those things. Just one of those moments in time when a bunch of baldheaded women hear a tune, and, simultaneously, are reminded what they're in it for, and what's in it for them.

And the sweetness of that fantasy, so real to each and every girl, so precious in that place so far from home, was so inviting that the bunch became involved in it. And the Buddhist Nun Corps de Ballet, led by Sergeant Wentworth, told the story of the good-hearted whore turned woodcutter until Johnny Mercer reached his crescendo, and the music began to dwindle. One by one, they dropped to the ground, their bald heads bent, their arms folded over their chain saws, like a featherless flock of dead orange swans.

During the performance, Ho Chi Binh, father of Ho Chi Minh, hamlet chief of An Hui, and a man who spent his life sweating, stepped back from the treeline and, without taking his eyes off the pirouetting body of Dinah Wentworth, snarled, "Disgusting! Revolting! Immoral! That woman is cavorting in the robes of the Buddha! You can see her naked body right through the cloth—I cannot believe such sacrilege!"

"Neither can I," said Tu Do, who had moved down the treeline to get a better look. "Neither can I."

Ho Chi Binh stamped his foot. "It is clearly some sect from the north. First it was the Cao Dais. Then the French with their Catholicism. Then the Communists with no respect for gods whatsoever. And now this. Well, the ancestors won't stand for it. It's trouble. What are they—Japanese?"

Tu Do thought for a moment. "No," he said, "I remember the Japanese. They were all very short. Ao Dai says they're Americans."

"No, not Americans," Ho Chi Binh sneered. "They're having too much fun. And not French, their hips are too wide. Well, I don't know what they are, but I know this: Their presence here means disharmony for the entire hamlet. And as hamlet chief, I intend to run them out. Especially that one." Ho Chi Binh pointed a moist, fat finger at Dinah. "Oh, I'd like to take a cane to that woman! Shameless! Look what she's doing! Oh, I can't. I just can't."

"So I hear," said Tu Do matter-of-factly.

"What do you mean?" demanded Ho Chi Binh. "Oh, never mind. I know what you mean. Yes, I get no thanks for trying to uphold the morals of An Hui. None whatsoever. And it isn't easy during a war, let me tell you. The youth think they own the place. Nothing old matters. My own son is a Communist. He doesn't worship ancestors, he tells me, he worships the hamlet, whatever that means.

"I brought him up. I saved his little body from the bombs. I hid his soul from that Virgin Mary. All right. Yes. I named him after Ho Chi Minh, but it was the path of least resistance, anyone could see that. And now he's grown, and what? He worships air, words, what is it?

"I asked him last week, 'Do you know that when I pass into the afterlife, I will be surrounded by angry people? Do you care?' And do you know what he said? 'Father, it's inevitable.' 'It's inevitable.' Can you believe it, Tu Do? Even you know nothing is inevitable."

"I'm no longer so sure," Tu Do muttered. He shook his grizzled head, and focused his beady eyes again, just in case.

There among the cartons stood a little goddess actually shorter than he. She was holding a small, round jar into which, periodically, she would dip her tiny finger, and then rub it slowly along the outline of her Perfect Mouth. She seemed to be in charge, for she did not join in the dance. She stood by, rubbing her Perfect Mouth, and watching in amusement.

Finally, she set down the jar and opened one of the boxes. From it, she removed, one by one, a number of gracefully shaped, dark-colored bottles.

"Oh," said Tu Do haltingly, "oh, oh, I think it's liquor. It is. It is. White liquor with bubbles. The French used to drink it.

And she is the keeper of it—the one with the Perfect Mouth! Oh, thank you, Ma A Phien, thank you!" Tu Do fell to his knees.

"What are you talking about, Tu Do?" Ho Chi Binh bristled with annoyance. "Why are you crying?"

"Last Thursday," said Tu Do through his tears, "I prayed to Ma A Phien, the Opium Ghost, for a death in the pleasures. I think my prayers have been answered."

"Well, that's it!" cried Ho Chi Binh in a fury. "That's the final outrage! I will fight back this time. I will fight against this moral decay if I have to fight alone. I am going to get my cane, and when I return, I will make *her* the example to all!"

Ho Chi Binh snarled pugnaciously in the direction of Dinah, and hurried off toward An Hui. Left to himself, Tu Do wiped away his tears. He took a swig of rice wine and began to dream of the things he could do to the Perfect Mouth of Major Lincoln-Pruitt. He could hardly wait for nightfall.

PHASE II: SEDUCTION

It was the Hour of the Cock, on the Day of the Cock, and Firebase Fox was sitting pretty. Okay, sir. Let's get some, sir. Here we go. That's 8:00 P.M. Western Mean Time on the 9th. A day unfavorable for burials, but good for commercial dealings, construction, and long, long voyages.

The predominant element was Fire. That's Fire, as in Foxy Fire. What a coincidence! East meets West. And the moon, well, the moon was beginning to rise over the strangest Hallmark card you ever saw.

Take her up, now. Take up that point of view like in a dream, and look down on twenty of the cutest hootches ever built. All in a sweet little horseshoe, just like that. Woven latania fronds for roofs, with pink plastic raincoats over them just in case of storms.

Do you see the pagoda? The queen did a great job—he really did. Eight foot high, six tiers, and covered all 'round with leopards fucking Buddha, up the ass. Faggot humor, man. They're still laughing in the prop room.

Do you see the women gathered there? Like a bunch of petal-picked daisies from above, so fragile and limbless. He loves me—he loves me not—he loves me—he loves me not. Where does it end?

Take her down, now. Take her down slowly, slowly, level with the doorways. One after another, the lava lamps sit on those white fur rugs, burbling those big red globs, like some art conception of the menstrual cycle.

Did you know that in the Tao, the male principle is associated with light and life, and the female principle with darkness and death? Now if that ain't a self-fulfilling prophecy, Charlie, what is?

Night dripped onto LZ My Sinh as if some celestial force were pouring out a jar of hot, black honey. The air was sticky and sweet, and the thighs of the women stuck together like muffins to an ungreased muffin pan. Zinnia was pacing back and forth in front of the pagoda.

"God, it's hot. I hate having sex when it's this hot and humid—the sweat runs in rivers and your skin makes embarrassing smacking noises—"

"Please, don't mention it." Fantasy was perched on a tree root. "I'm this close to getting cystitis as we speak. I guess it's the female equivalent of jungle rot. Please God, don't let me get it. Every time I travel, damn. Last year I went to London. I was barely off the plane and zap!"

Mandy was sitting in the lotus position on the ground, fanning herself with her human-hair purse. "It's funny. I don't know whether to hope for a handsome guy or not. It'd be a shame to waste a handsome guy."

"Hey!" Zinnia stopped in front of Mandy. "They're gooks, not guys, okay? Let's get that straight."

"Listen, sister!" Mandy was indignant. "You're the one who brought up sex. I mean, we do intend to sleep with them, or are we calling it something else?"

"Infiltrating," said Zinnia and began pacing again.

One by one, the women of the platoon were sauntering into the hearth area. They milled around and chatted, waiting for the appearance of Major Lincoln-Pruitt.

"You know," said Mandy, the brightness of her voice slicing through the humid air, "they say if someone kills you when you're coming, it's the best orgasm in the world."

"Who says that? Men?" Fantasy's tone was sarcastically sweet.

Mandy laughed. "Yeah, *touché*. Men. Or not men. There are no men anymore, just slope-eyed dicks."

"On the other hand," said Fantasy, "when you put it that way, who wants to sleep with them?"

"Yes, that's our problem," laughed Dinah as she strutted into the hearth area and began lighting the candles on the pagoda altar. "The Viet Cong are at once our mortal enemies and the future lovers for whom we have gussied up so long. The hookers in the platoon, Mandy and my girls, have some inkling of how this works."

"Sure." Mandy glanced conspiratorially at the other women. "Why, any shrink could tell you that tonight I am going to make reality of my deepest fantasy. I hope it doesn't end too quick. I could use a good screw."

The women gathered around, snickering and nodding in agreement.

"Great," said Fantasy. "Where does that leave me, Zinnia, and the Major?"

"On the same trip in a different boat, honey," said Mandy. "But I hasten to point out that fantasy is not reality—i.e., none of us has killed a man before. Am I right? Has anyone here ever killed a man?"

"No, but I've kissed a cockatoo," said Zinnia.

The women laughed and muttered among themselves, until Major Lincoln-Pruitt ripped into the hearth area like a human gyroscope and, within seconds, dispelled their thoughts and seized their concentration.

The tiny commander stood in the doorway, surveying her troops. Her straight little body twinkled in the light of the votive candles. Her round, dolly eyes stretched open with excitement and power. In one little hand, she clutched a green rabbit's foot, her piece of luck, with which she gestured as she spoke, pawing the meaning on the heavy, humid air.

"Women of the Foxy Fire platoon, I commend you. The camp you have built is a masterpiece, perfect in every detail, truly a New Life Hamlet. Wentworth, you will take polaroids of it in the morning, to send back to the Joint Chiefs. They have never seen its like before. But perhaps, if all goes well tonight, they shall see its like again. Perhaps we will build another and another, until we have swept our way across Vietnam and won this war!"

The women cheered.

"Reconnaissance tells me we are surrounded. The enemy knows we are here and has known since early this afternoon. The fact that we are still alive, untouched by sniper fire or grenade burst, indicates that we have intrigued them. Phase I of the Foxy Fire Op, Illusion, has gone without a hitch. Our position is secured, ladies. Our loose policy has been a success!"

The women cheered again. Like a gang of carnival pinheads, their exuberance was at once frightening and adorable.

"All right." The Major silenced them with her rabbit paw. "All right. But let me warn you: Do not yourselves become enmeshed in the illusion we have spun. This is a war as serious as any you have waged between the bedposts of America. And as with any man you've ever had, your vulnerability on this LZ, your Achilles heel, is sub- submission." The Major stuttered on the word. It was as difficult for her to speak it as to hear it. "Loss of self, pleasure in the skirmish. Remember: The muscles we use to fake orgasm are the muscles we use to kill, so lie on your backs and think of Hanoi or whatever it takes to get the job done. Do what you have to do to get those dicks up. You don't have to like it to do it, we all know that, and take a lesson from the boy-soldiers' mistakes over here and don't get involved.

"Okay. Phases II and III, Seduction and Revelation, are yet to come and require our full attention. After the briefing, you will return to your huts and begin the Seduction. Be sure that at all times you are visible through your doorway and from the treeline. Most likely the enemy will split up and seek one-on-one contact, at which point you are on your own and good luck to you. If they come en masse, we'll go into the party mode and you can choose the guy you want. No catfights please; the larger battle is what's important.

"Okay. Through tiny speakers with which I have just bugged every hut, I will know when each of you makes contact. As soon as everyone has a date, I will give the signal. Any time after that you can activate the Probe. Please kiss the enemy when you do this lest he cry out and alert the others. That done, sheathe the enemy in the body bag and wait for dawn, at which time I will summon the Pimp Cav."

The Major whooped. "Have you practiced your Vietnamese sweet talk?"

"We have!" the women shouted.

"Have you oiled the L.P.A.R.D.?"

"We have!" the women shouted again.

"Good! Any questions?"

"Do we have to kiss them, ma'am?" asked Mandy, clearly upset. " 'Cause it's against *my* Rules of Engagement to ever . . ."

"Yes, Rasmussen. As I said, if they cry out in pain, it could endanger the entire Op. Not kissing them is an offense tantamount to treason, and I will court-martial, so be warned. It's

for your own safety, Rasmussen, not their pleasure, try to remember that."

"Yeah, but they won't know that. Only I will know that."
Mandy pouted.

"That's correct. Self-sufficiency is what it's all about. Smith?"

"You cautioned us against achieving orgasms out of
pleasure?"

"Yes, Smith?"

"Well, is there something different about NVA guys—a special skill at foreplay that Ho Chi Minh teaches them? Because
under normal circumstances with an American guy it takes me
about an hour—that's with or without American aid—so I cannot imagine . . ."

"Hell," boomed Zinnia, "I might defect!"

The platoon hooted with laughter.

"You never know, Smith," said the Major, "you could luck
out. But from all we know, these gooks are relatively unsophis-
ticated sexually, innocent even. If you're warm, friendly, and
inviting, it should be a snap. Look, Charlie's the type of guy
who's always seeking a sanctuary. You can easily be it. Welcome him into your hot little Iron Triangle, and he will be
yours in perpetuity. Godspeed. You are dismissed."

At the edge of the footpath to LZ My Sinh, during the
crossover minutes between the hour of the Dog and the hour
of the Pig, Le Van Dong stood in the darkness, awaiting the
men of An Hui. All in all, twenty adult males would be going,
between the ages of seventeen and seventy, cadre members
and hamlet-dwellers alike, the entire viable male population.

There had been some trouble over the decision. Some of the
senior elders wished to go and just watch. Some of the younger
boys, seeing no need for a delegation, demanded an organized
grenade-throwing instead. The women of the hamlet were
frustrated and anxious. The thought of their husbands' visiting
a group of suspicious and half-clothed females caused them

worry. And though, surely, their opinions carried no weight in the Great Scheme of Things, they could cause commotion in the Small. Le had calmed them all.

"Suppose," he said, "they are Buddhist nuns. Sacred women of the temple. Innocent. Devoted. Serene. If we spy on them, kill them, or even ignore them, without knowing the purpose of their mission here, we will bring a curse upon our heads. And another curse the hamlet of An Hui does not need."

The hamlet dwellers knew he was right. For centuries, it seemed, An Hui had been, to the gods and ancestors who hovered by, even as a spitoon. The rice harvest, according to the oldest living memory, had always been meager. So meager that nowadays the phrase "our rice harvest" was used in the community to denote a dearth. If one wished to insult a man's lineage, one merely said, "Your mother was as fruitful as our rice harvest," and immediately there was litigation.

When it rained, it rained too much. Swelling the Oma River till it flooded. Creating a landscape so muddy and insect-rife, that most of the hamlet's inhabitants retired to their beds, under the mosquito netting, not to emerge 'till the rains were over.

When the sun shone, it brought drought. I was so hot, that to work in one's kitchen garden invited sunstroke. Husbands and wives who had not separated during the rains, often did so during the drought, claiming that the touch of another person's skin, in that kind of heat, was, without question, grounds for divorce.

Since the young women of the district hamlets refused to set foot in An Hui, its inhabitants were forced to intermarry. This practice had left them paranoid, cynical, and somewhat dim. Even the French had scorned them. Their women, said the colonists, were too ugly. Their men, too stupid. The French had plundered the hamlet of goods and taxes, converted whom they could, and then flounced out. They saw no point in building a lycée where no one even sensed the concept of chic.

Nobody cared about An Hui except the Communists. To them it was perfect, representative, an example for all of South Vietnam. And that is why they sent Le Van Dong, one of their foremost organizers, to attend as midwife in its ideological rebirth.

"The ancestors will never forgive you," Le continued. "So if, as I believe, your lack of communal spirit and your hunger for individual wealth is what has caused their anger, and your misery, then slaughtering a crowd of unarmed women will, undoubtedly, be the last yarrow stalk. Let us go and see what is what, and tomorrow we will discuss it again."

The women of An Hui were placated. The location and hour of departure were fixed at the crossover of Dog and Pig, at the start of the My Sinh footpath, where, now, Le Van Dong was planning the strategy.

"Their hamlet," Le was saying, "is accessible on all sides. Each hut has a doorway facing the treeline, and there is no barrier hedge and, therefore, no apparent obstacle to our entry. I should think," he added pointedly for the benefit of Ao Dai, who was standing sullenly on the edge of the crowd, "this is but one more indication of their desire for peaceful interaction."

"Or the immensity of their cunning," Ao Dai snapped in retort.

"As you wish," said Le angrily. "We will approach in a group. Then, once at the treeline, we will part and seek individual contact. Each of you will interrogate the woman you have chosen. When you are satisfied you have gotten from her everything that you can, return to An Hui to engage in further discussion."

The men nodded in agreement, and Ao Dai stamped her foot.

"Ridiculous!" she sneered. "If it is a trick, one by one you will be easily overcome. Your only chance is as a mob. It is just because they are women that you are being so foolish. It is just because they are women that . . ."

"Leave us, Ao Dai," said Le with barely concealed fury. And in explanation for this, his first deviation from the principle of free and equal discourse and dissension, added, "At certain times of the lunar cycle, even Communist women should stay indoors."

The men laughed, and Ao Dai fled down the footpath and into the night.

"Is everyone armed?" asked Le. The men held up a motley selection of M16s, AK-47s, farm implements, and canes.

"Good," said Le. "Let Buddha, the ancestors, and Ho Chi Minh smile favorably upon our mission. Let us go."

The men crept along the footpath, entombed in leaves and blackness. The only light came from a half-full moon which dribbled through the trees, and sparkled on the metal of the gunbarrels. When they reached the LZ, Le gave the order. "Spread out," he whispered, and the men did.

"I'm coming, Ma A Phien," said Tu Do softly, and he scurried toward the hootch of Major Lincoln-Pruitt.

Corporal Mandy Rasmussen was in a panic. Her lava lamp had broken. Somewhere there had been a short and it had gone out, all of a sudden. The big red globules slowly sank to the bottom of the cone, maybe like, God forbid, an omen of things to come.

Trembling, she grabbed for her human-hair purse, and removed from it the six scented candles she always carried with her, just in case. She surveyed the hut frantically, searching for flat surfaces, but the Shrine of the Soil remained the only place she could put them.

It sat in the eastern corner of her hut: a little wooden altar, not unlike a vanity table she had made once in eleventh-grade carpentry class. On it stood a square dime-store mirror, used, the Major had told them, by the Vietnamese to ward off evil spirits. She prayed it would ward them off now.

Centered above the mirror was the picture of the Buddha they'd been issued, a few prayer strips, and two votive candles, which she hurriedly lit. Around this arrangement, the Major said, they could put whichever ancestors they cared to propitiate, whoever might inspire them in their mission.

Mandy had chosen Jimi Hendrix. A really nice photo she had snipped out of a magazine, where the light was very blue, and he was playing the guitar so hard, it seemed like any minute his brains might explode from the effort of sheer involvement.

Next to it was a snap of Bobby Satin, all dressed up in his new fur coat, taken the day of the big snow, by the polar bear cage in Central Park. Then, a little, tiny picture, an old fifties Kodak with serrated edges, black and white, of the wood-frame house in Hopkins. And in the midst of all, right above the Buddha, a purple pennant from the Minnesota Vikings.

With great care, Mandy attached the six candles to the altar surface and lit them. Instantly, she felt better. But for a while there, it had been touch and go, and she knew it.

She had tried all her life to conquer it. She had made the mental journey back to the primal source over and over again. She had soothed herself with logic every step of the way, facing the terror, and even laughing at its Freudian gaudiness. But it did no good. At twenty-three, she remained deathly afraid of the dark.

Safe in the light of the scented candles, she went over it again now. Therapy. After all, in her line of work it was a handicap. A lot of guys liked it with the lights off, and because she would never turn a trick in the dark, she'd lost money. Bobby never knew. She always made her trap. But because of the fear, she'd had to really hustle. It was not practicality, but freedom from the anguish that drove her now to relive it.

It begins when Mandy is six and her father takes her ice-fishing on Lake Minnetonka. He has an icehouse there, a little wooden shack in the center of the lake, with a chimney on top. They drive by once and she sees it: a grown-up playhouse, and she wants to go so badly and play there. Her mother says it's boring, and all he does there is fish through a hole in the ice. But she knows better. She knows about playhouses. Maybe he has dollies and games there, or maybe something special that only fathers have and they could play with it together. So she begs and begs and one day when her mother is at bridge club, her father takes her ice-fishing.

On the way, they stop at the liquor store. You have to have whiskey, her father says, to keep warm. It's a long walk across the ice, and she carries the bait—long, squirmy worms and hunks of fishflesh. She is very nervous lest they get out of the bag and crawl up her arms and into her mouth, or worse, lest she might drop them and ruin them. But they didn't, and she didn't, and she is very proud.

Inside the little house, there is a black wood stove, a hurricane lamp, two chairs, and a scruffy place in the ice where an old ice hole has frozen over. It is cold. The walls are covered with pasted-up pictures of girls with no clothes on. They all smile sweetly. Nudists, her father explains when she inquires about them.

He builds a fire in the stove. Then he drills a hole in the ice, attaches the bait to the hook, and begins to fish and drink whiskey. She watches him. She sits in the chair and sniffs her hair, and when she tries to speak to him, he shushes her. The sound of her voice, he says, will scare away the fish.

All day she sits in silence, trying not to fidget, or get in the way, or even exist. She stares at the nudists on the wall, getting to know them one by one, giving them names.

It is getting dark now in the little house, but he seems not to notice. She wants to tell him, but she is afraid that the sound of her voice will scare away the fish and he will be angry.

Suddenly, he falls out of his chair and onto the ice floor. The liquor in the bottle he is holding spills and forms a puddle. She shakes him, but he will not get up. She shouts at him, but his eyes do not open.

She runs out onto the lake, but it is dark and everyone has gone. She stands on the vast expanse of ice, shivering in her pink snowsuit, and cries. Then she goes back inside.

She does not know how to light the hurricane lamp. She does not know how to keep the fire going. Soon, there is nothing but black and cold. Every night, the nudists go through this, she thinks to herself; they must be very brave.

Huddled next to her snoring father, rigid with fear in the icy blackness, she waits for morning. When it comes, he wakes and drives her home. I have a hangover, he says, and nothing more.

Her mother throws her pink snowsuit in the trash. It smells like Jack Daniels, her mother tells her, very angry. She cannot understand this, she tells her mother, there was no one else with them. They were all alone, except for the nudists.

"Nudists," said Mandy, laughing to herself. "Nudists, for Christ's sake." And then a sound at the doorway made her look up.

Le Van Dong stood on the doorsill, his AK-47 Kalashnikov rifle cradled in his hands, the candleglow highlighting his features like one of those Hollywood 8×10 glossies from the 1940s.

For the first time in years, Mandy smiled involuntarily, out of pure and simple delight. A lovely heat spread through her body and brain as, very slowly, she approached Le and looked into his eyes.

"Good evening," she said in Vietnamese. "Would you like to come in?"

"Yes," said Le, quite beside himself.

"What's your name?" asked Mandy, unable to move, her body pinioned in the force field of this young man's magnetism.

"Le Van Dong," he replied, handing her his rifle.

"Really?" she asked, looking down at the weapon, not understanding.

"Oh," he said, realizing what he had done and taking back

the rifle. "That's odd. I don't know why I . . ." And he laughed.
"My name's Mandy," she said, laughing too. He nodded,
pleasure illuminating his features.

"I know," he said.

Sergeant Fantasy Smith was reclining on the flokati, listening to Frank Sinatra, and throwing the I Ching. Her question
was: Will the Foxy Fire Op be a success? She would have
liked to ask something more specific like: Will I be alive by the
end of the night? But with the I Ching, you never really got a
straight answer, and something of that importance, left to your
own interpretation, could get truly depressing. So she stuck to
the general, and she threw 51 CHEN/THE AROUSING (Shock,
Thunder).

The Judgment read:

> Shock brings success.
> Shock comes—oh, oh!
> Laughing words—ha, ha!
> The shock terrifies for a hundred miles,
> And he does not let fall the sacrificial
>   spoon and chalice.

Well, that sounded true enough. It was going to be a shock,
poor lambs, though only God knew what that part about the
sacrificial spoon meant. She had a six at the top. It read:

> Shock brings ruin and terrified gazing around.
> Going ahead brings misfortune.
> If it has not yet touched one's own body
> But has reached one's neighbor first,
> There is no blame.
> One's comrades have something to talk about.

Okay. Of course there was going to be ruin and terror; this
was war, after all, men were going to die. But it wasn't going
to touch her own body first, please God, and so there was no
blame and afterwards all the girls would have cocktails in Da

Nang and talk about it. She did not like that part about bringing misfortune, but basically it was a good reading, and there
was nothing really to worry about.

Feeling calmer now, Fantasy raised herself off the flokati,
and in her slow, languid way, meandered toward her Shrine of
the Soil. Perched on the altar, next to a copy of the score from
Pal Joey which she was learning for dinner-theater work in the
future, was a large publicity shot of Bob Hope with a line of
go-go-booted dancing girls behind him. She was third from the
left with a little too much cleavage showing. But, Mr. Hope
maintained, that was the least we could do for our fighting
men, and she couldn't have agreed more. The photo was taken
in Cam Ranh Bay, on board some aircraft carrier, before she
met the Major, before the Foxy Fire Op and the L.P.A.R.D.,
before she herself . . .

It was funny to think of being at war, of having the mandate
to kill. In America, women never did. Men hogged it like they
hogged everything else. In Asia, Woman the Destroyer was
part of the deity, but in the U.S. they didn't want to hear of
that; it only made men nervous. Holy women were virgins, not
killers, and let's not discuss it further. Of course a man could
throw grenades better, no denying that. She couldn't throw
worth a damn, forget heavy grenades or pipe bombs. No,
women should do what women do best, and with the
L.P.A.R.D. you make war from behind, or on top, or through
the tip of the tongue or finger, as well as in the missionary
position. There was creativity involved. It wasn't just a dumb
jock thing of jacking off a big metal penis.

"Hands up!" Ho Chi Minh burst into her hut, trained his
K-50 submachine gun between her breasts, and screamed
shrilly.

Fantasy jumped and threw up her hands in terror. "God,
you scared the life out of me," she gasped in Vietnamese.
"Relax, man. Nothing is worth getting so crazed about. I'm
unarmed. Really. Look around." She ran her almond eyes all

over the very young, very scared Vietnamese man before her. He didn't budge, but stared, seemingly hypnotized, back at her. "That is a fabulous, fabulous gun," she cooed, running her finger along the barrel. "Do you shoot tigers with this?"

"One," stammered Ho, gloriously confused now. "God," said Fantasy, glancing wistfully toward the forest, "I'd do just about anything for a tiger coat. Just about anything." Fantasy smiled her most effective audition smile, the one she used to get the part in *Two for the Seesaw*. And as she watched Ho's neck muscles relax in the seeming openness of her gaze, she wondered if she would walk differently afterwards, if, like losing your virginity, men would be able to tell what she'd done simply by the way she moved.

Master Sergeant Dinah Wentworth was ready. She had taken a Seconal, downed a few glasses of champagne, and was nearly dressed. God, how she hated those fucking saffron robes, but they were the uniform and, by Christ, it was her duty to wear them!

She leaned over her Shrine of the Soil and peered at herself in the mirror. "Dinah!" Her Welsh accent cuddled her words. "You look like shit bald. Like a badly painted, thousand-year-old Easter egg. And let me say this: You are nothing without a garter belt. Nothing. Zero. Limp dick. Get it on, girl, get it on. You need all the help you can get."

Her rucksack was sitting on the altar. Very carefully and covertly, she took from it one black-lace garter belt, one pair of black nylons, two stiletto-toed, six-inch-heeled black boots, and a small black whip.

"My tricks of the trade," she mumbled as she pulled on the nylons. "What I'm famous for—renowned throughout the corporate structures of the corn belt. I won't work without a net." She laced up her boots. "And nobody's going to make me!"

She peered in the mirror again. "There. Much better. A fighting chance. Oh, my secret love." She caught sight of the photo of the Major pinned by the Army-issue Buddha. "I'm doing this for you, Vic. So you can have your due. So they can't fuck you over like they fucked me and I was thanking them for it. Thank you, sir. My pleasure, sir. Come again." She cracked her little whip less for effect than to bring herself to. "It's a goddam business, nobody understands that but you, Vic. It's time to work—she works. What? Do I need to apologize for it? Never! As God is my witness—"

She heard a noise behind her and she froze. In the mirror she could see Ho Chi Binh standing in the doorway. His sweaty, fat face was smug with rage. His cane was raised menacingly above his head. Hardly moving, she drew from her rusksack a black, leather hangman's mask. She slipped it down over her face, zipped the zipper across her mouth, and whipped around.

"Put down that cane!" she snapped in Vietnamese. "Put it down!"

He did so. She marched over to where he stood, took the cane, and shoved him to his knees with it.

"You've been a very naughty boy," she said, "and I'm afraid you'll have to be punished."

Captain Zinnia Jackson was tripping. She had eaten the sugar cube just after the briefing. It was, she knew, the only way she could stand sitting in that claustrophobic hut without going off.

Her blood began to undulate beneath her skin, and she got the sweats. The largeness of her body was overwhelming her. Her hands, her feet, her breasts. Man, she did not know how she had grown so big. Like something in a Japanese movie. Like a man.

"And shit," she thought to herself, "here I am doing a man's job again. I don't know how this happened, but I don't like it." The last thing she remembered was graduating from Smith in a white dress on a clover-sweet lawn, and the next thing she knew she was dropped in a Vietnamese jungle and told she would have to fuck her way out, or die. Oh Lord, she could hardly wait to get back to civilian life. In the future, no one could stop her as long as she was packing the Leopard. No one. No man. "Shit." She was getting depressed. "War's a man's damn job. And they can't even do that right. I could just . . ."

No. She pulled her thoughts away. No. She should do something wise with her time. She reached for the box of body paint.

She took out the tiny jars and fixated on her thigh. "Zinnia, honey, there ain't an ounce of landowner in you anywhere." She rummaged through the box again and found the paintbrush.

Black canvas. What can I be? Something Asian that's black.

She tripped for a moment and what surfaced behind her eyes was a photo she'd seen in *Life Magazine*. A cloud leopard. A black cloud leopard with pure, gold spots and long black whiskers. "That's it. That's who I really am."

Slowly, she unscrewed the jar of gold paint, dipped the brush in the swirling liquid, and applied it to her thigh. It was cool and feathery, and the paint seemed to sink on through to her thighbone. She twirled the paintbrush round and round and round.

A thousand thoughts later, an old Vietnamese man with a kindly face, and straggly white hair in a bun at the nape of his neck, materialized at her doorway. In his hand he was holding a sickle.

For a long time, Zinnia stared at him, trying to remember some Vietnamese. Then, for some acid-induced reason, she crawled on all fours over to the door, looked up at him, and growled.

"I am a tiger," she said in his language, not knowing the word for cloud leopard. "Please don't kill me."

Tran Van Luc looked down at her in amazement.

"I couldn't," he said softly, leaning his sickle against the doorjamb. "In An Hui, the tiger is sacred."

Major Victoria Lincoln-Pruitt was sitting at her Shrine of the Soil addressing the battered photo of her father and General MacArthur.

"This moment, gentlemen," she was saying, "is, quite simply, the pinnacle of my career. The culmination of a lifelong battle against male stupidity and domination. To you both, I dedicate this—the final phase of the Foxy Fire Op. To Revelation, gentlemen!"

With a resounding pop, she uncorked a bottle of champagne, and toasted her paternal ancestor and his comrade-at-arms.

In the corner, the little speaker crackled with static. She listened as, one by one, the women of her platoon made contact with the enemy. "Good," she murmured. "Very good. It should be any time now." She glanced toward the doorway of her hut, but, as yet, there was no one there.

She turned back to the photo and remembered the day, months ago, when she had attended with her mentor, General Larson, a top-secret meeting at the Pentagon. A meeting at which it was perfectly clear that American boys were losing the war in Southeast Asia.

One of the Joint Chiefs suggested that perhaps some hangover influence from the French was rubbing off on the troops and causing their lethargy, but nobody knew for sure. American boys were bitter and unpatriotic, energyless and sullen. They forgot to wear their flak jackets. They deserted and became addicted to drugs. They cracked under fire and committed atrocities that could not be attributed to the pressures of battle. Oh, there were instances of bravery. But they were deemed acts of insanity within the ranks, and the brave men responsible, puppets and fools.

It was at this dismal proceeding that the Major presented

her plan. "Forget the boys," she said. "With the right weapon a random squad of barely liberated women can win this war." There was, of course, laughter around the table.

"You laugh," she said, "but consider this: For eons women have destroyed men. They have sapped their creative fluids, befuddled the clarity of their minds, and made of their intensity of purpose, a senseless mockery. And how? Through sex. Through a perfection in it. Through the withholding of it. By being the one who'll put out or the one who never has. Or in between. It doesn't matter. It's simple, basic, a fact of life and the founding principle upon which I have based the design of the ultimate women's weapon. Generals," she said, "I give you the Lincoln-Pruitt Anti-Rape Device."

She distributed a Xerox of the design, and continued with her explanation. "Originally I conceived it as a defensive armament, but I soon realized the submissiveness that implied. Long years of male brainwashing had made me forget, once again, that the defensive and the offensive are parts of a whole, yin and yang as it were. It has never depended on who's on top." The Joint Chiefs, though loath to agree, did not interrupt.

"The L.P.A.R.D. has given rape a new meaning," she went on. "And for this reason, is the long-sought-for answer to the problems of female combat. Not only does it remove from the female soldier's mind the helpless terror of rape, and its concomitant submissive attitudes and postures, it actually places her in the position of being eager for intercourse with the enemy. With the L.P.A.R.D., for the first time women will be able to kill easily and fully, and with complete security that no one will be taking obscene polaroids of them after the battle. Guns are clearly for men, but the Leopard is for a woman." The Joint Chiefs winced, but they recognized her logic as invincible.

"The strategy is clear. It involves the female soldier's most natal talent: the seduction of man. In the case of war, the seduction of the enemy. How do we accomplish this in Vietnam? Well," she said, "not with a jackboot, Generals. Nor with a mortar shell, nor one of your discreet bursts of napalm. But with sensitivity, poise, and good grooming. By dropping like manna from heaven, dressed as refugee Buddhist nuns, and creating in the enemy's midst, an illusion so inviting and warm, so familiar and yet so new, that like a piece of candy proffered by a stranger, any fear and suspicion of motive is swept away in the desire to taste the sweet.

"It is a matter of sensitivity, Generals. Of knowing what is done and not done, and using that knowledge to your advantage. This is not the fifteenth century, and the Vietnamese are not Mayans. The white man with a gun is no longer a god." She paused for a moment to let this sink in.

"The white woman, however, seemingly helpless, her weapon hidden from sight in the place she is most known to be vulnerable, remains, thanks to men like you, a goddess to us all and the means by which we can win the war in Vietnam."

She had proposed the Operation in detail then. It was, of course, unassailable and instantly accepted as part of the Phoenix Program.

The Major looked closely at the two men in the battered photo. "Well, Father, General, it is the moment of truth and we are in the East. And in the East, if one's mission is to be a success, one's ancestors must smile favorably upon it. And so I ask you both for your support in this undertaking. That the Foxy Fire Op might live, a credit to the very freedoms for which so many young men under you, fought and died."

The Major bowed her head for a moment, and then looked up at her doorway. Still, there was no one there. She came close to panic. Any time now, the others would be ready to activate the Probe, to test the weapon—her weapon. They would be waiting for her to give the signal, her, their leader, their archetype, their energy source. And what if she had to give that signal without ever knowing the thrill of the ground attack, the satisfaction of her personal penetration capability? She would be left unassimilated. Unable ever to assess her own ability to mount, sustain, and execute a serious offensive action. "Victoria, Victoria," she ordered herself, "calm down. Calm down now. You're acting like a woman who's waiting for a blind date who's late. He'll be here. Don't worry. He'll be here."

She studied her face in the mirror and curled her lashes with an eyelash curler. Even bald, she did look like Edith Piaf. She was an older woman who'd be young forever, and rich, if the anti-rape device proved effective, and famous as a savior of women's souls. Victoria Lincoln-Pruitt: The Woman Who Won the War in Vietnam. The panic left her, and once more she was suffused with the commander's desire to gain the military objective.

"And what of children?" The voice of her dead mother snaked up from the past and levitated by her eardrum, causing a gnaw of anguish in the region of what Army doctors had long ago diagnosed as a duodenal ulcer. She reached in her rucksack for the Gelusil bottle and sucked on it like a starving infant. And what of children? the voice asked again. "Oh Ma," her thoughts began, "you know the Leopard is my child. It's my invention, my baby." The voice shuddered. "Don't even say that, Victoria. That *thing* is no substitute for a husband and children. If anything, it's kept you from it. What man wants a woman who's obsessed with making her diaphragm into a lethal weapon? What man . . ."

Tu Do chose this moment to trip over the Major's doorsill and fall flat on his face in the middle of her flokati rug. The bottle of rice wine he was carrying, in lieu of a weapon, spun out of his hand and smashed against the wall of the hut.

The Major, startled, struck a karate pose, and then, realizing what had happened, peered down at him as he scrambled and lurched to his feet.

When he had regained his full height of five feet, the Major noted that despite the fact he was sodden with drink, his sexual organ was pushing against his pants. A good sign. A very good sign. It would be easy.

"Not him?" the voice asked. "Victoria, not a bum, a derelict, a wino?"

She raised her glance from his erect organ to his bulbous face with its leering grin and its grizzly, razor-burning stubble, and the smell of his unwashed body pervaded the hootch and her consciousness. And then, for the first time since she had conceived the L.P.A.R.D., and then the Foxy Fire Op, and through all the training and planning that had led up to this encounter, for the first time she was hit with the reality: In order to kill this drunken sod, first she would have to punk him.

PHASE III: REVELATION

At the edge of the treeline, in front of the hut of Corporal Mandy Rasmussen, Ao Dai stood within a grove of bamboo trees and wept. Through her tears she saw Mandy doing things to Le that she had only dreamed of. Every kiss, every stroke and lick sent through her body a spasm of anguish. For what had never been, for what, now, never could be, and most of all for her own paralyzing inability to express her love, she pounded her fists against the slender bamboo and sobbed.

It was the fault of the war, and of her mother and her father, of her culture, the French, and the Americans. She threw herself to the forest floor and writhed in pain. "Oh no," she moaned. "Oh Le, oh love." She rooted in the hot earth beneath her, and mourned the passing of all she had hoped for.

"No kitchen garden with frail, green seedlings I could nurture to fruition. No . . . no round-faced, cheery babies with bows in their hair and tiny, red shoes. No . . . no handsome, young, Communist-organizer husband to shoo my fears. No."

Somewhere near the bamboo grove a radio cackled and sputtered, and Ao Dai shrank in silence. Her woman's tears were sucked, as through a vacuum, back, deep into that innermost sorrow pit beneath her rib cage. Like a desiccated leaf, she blended with the forest floor, and listened intently.

An American voice spoke softly somewhere in the forest behind her.

"This is Avenger Corps. Recon A-OK. We are at Firebase Fox. Over."

"Report Avenger. We hear you. Over."

"Affirmative on the slit platoon. They are in active service. Over."

"No shit? Over."

"Charles is clearing his weapon, sir, jacking a full clip into one of our pieces. I'm lookin' right at it. Over."

"Fuck the 1st Cav. We'll never live this down. Over."

"Can we mop 'em? Over."

"Negative, Avenger. We got plans. Return to base. Over."

"Sir. Is there any mention of this in the Rules of Engagement, sir? Over."

"No, but it's definitely cheating, son. Return to base. Over and out."

Ao Dai was stunned. Though she did not understand the language, she knew the sound of those voices only too well. Marines! American Marines! She had been right all along. The women were American aggressors! Their presence on the LZ was a grisly trick! They were to lure the men into their huts and then the Marines would surround them and kill them! How clever. How cunning. Only another woman could have seen through it, and who would believe her? Her intelligence would be ascribed to jealousy of the women's beauty. Her astuteness to envy of their poise. She had to get to Le before it was too late! Ao Dai leapt to her feet and grabbed her rifle, but before she could run, a huge male hand clamped over her mouth, and another between her legs, and she was dragged, kicking and struggling, into the underbrush.

"Look," the Major was saying in flawless Vietnamese, "it could have happened to anyone who's had as much rice wine as you've obviously had, you know." She was on her hands and knees scrubbing at the flokati. "Of course it would have been more convenient if you could have made it outside, but that's the Tao." The Major heaved the smelly kleenexes out the doorway and as she did so, snuck a look at the circle of hootches. All was quiet and cozy. Warm webs of light emanated from the entrances. While Tu Do was throwing up, she had given the signal: a throaty ululation of the Buddhist prayer for propitious rebirth. He had never noticed. Phase III, Revelation, was underway.

She turned back, smiling, to the vomit-covered Buddha plopped on her rug. "Well," she said brightly, noticing with horror that the nausea had made him lose his erection, "let's clean you up." She kneeled down next to him and wiped off his jowly face and ragged shirt. Tu Do stared at her soft, glossy lips and wondered drunkenly how he could get around to violating them. He giggled and then, placing his hand over hers, guided it from his shoulder to the organ in repose in his lap. She checked her desire to look into his eyes and, against her will, began to squeeze him.

Fifteen minutes later the bursitis in her shoulder began to throb, one leg fell asleep, and still nothing had happened. She was not getting the cobra out of the basket this way, that much was clear. She stopped squeezing and looked at him questioningly. The turnip's eyes twinkled with delight. Reddening with embarrassment but undaunted, he pointed to her lips and then to his lap.

"What?" murmured the Major, trying to understand the gesture. "You want me to what?" She rose from the flokati and staggered to her altar, dragging one awakening leg behind her. Oral sex. She poured more champagne. He wanted her to perform oral sex on him. It was her mission, her patriotic duty, and yet, and yet. . . . You don't have to like it to do it, isn't that what she told the platoon? Make up whatever story you want for yourself, just get the job done. Okay. But what if he were in the seven percent Dinah mentioned? She would be there for hours, lapping at him as if she were some mindless whitecap, and at the end of it all, the possibility that she would be no closer to Revelation than she was now.

Though she admitted it to no one, she had never had oral sex in her life. Once, a long time ago in Cambridge, she had tried it with a preppie from a good family. He sat on the edge of the bed, a stocky blond guy naked except for a pink La Coste shirt, and she couldn't go through with it. For years afterward the La Coste alligator reminded her of this scene and symbolized her sexual hysteria. And if she couldn't stand it with a guy who had six generations of Boston aristocracy trapped in his jism, she doubted that a Vietnamese wino would do the trick. No! She had never had oral sex in her life, and even to stem the red tide of Communist aggression, even to stop the flip-flop of dominoes all over Southeast Asia, she did not intend to start now!

"You want a drink?" she asked, glancing over her shoulder. Tu Do's lustful eyes widened and he nodded eagerly. She turned back to the altar. Well, what else could she do? She could French-kiss him. She could lie down next to him, press her lips to his and thrust her tongue down his—no. There was no chance that she was going to do that, and even if she did, there was no guarantee—look, Major, she told herself sharply, there's never any guarantee. The power of your Seduction is your guarantee as you planned it. As you trained for it.

She was completely turned off. Her brain cut production of the sex hormone and no fantasy seemed able to reactivate it. She stood before her altar and understood that she was not capable of seducing this man. She would not stroke him again. She would never kiss him. There was only one thing left to do. From beneath her watch crystal, she removed a tiny packet of white powder and dumped it in a paper cup. She then poured in the champagne, stirred it with her finger, turned around and handed it to Tu Do. She watched expectantly as he slurped the bubbly liquid down his throat.

The apothecary in Hong Kong had said it would take one minute, tops. It was the best you could buy, the purest, illegal, and very expensive. But, he swore, it worked and had done for centuries throughout Asia. She had threatened him with her MPs, but it had not fazed him. "No worry," he said. "Look. I show."

He called in an ancient and very soiled beggar who was sitting with a rice bowl and a monkey in front of the shop. They spoke in Chinese, some money changed hands, and he gave the old man the powder in a glass of tea. "Watch," he said, pointing to the beggar's crotch.

In seconds, the man's aged, scaly organ began to rise as if by levitation. The head snuck through the fly in his pajamas like a cartoon mouse in search of cheese. The monkey grabbed onto it, chucking and squealing, and created, in the dusty, cluttered shop, some pandemonium as the anguished beggar sought, frantically, to release his manhood from the furry, simian grip. The apothecary laughed heartily, and beat at the monkey with his ornamental cane. Finally, it fled, screeching and grunting, and settled on top of a glass ginger jar containing a fetal duck. "Rhino horn." The Chinese apothecary grinned. "Never fail. You have fun." And she paid him five hundred American dollars in cash, for a single, precious gram.

Suddenly Tu Do's penis was, to his astonishment, fully erect. Without warning, the Major kicked him in the jaw, pinned him to the rug, spread her legs, and, with the oil from the L.P.A.R.D. as a gooey catalyst, impaled herself. She then squeezed her pubococcyneal muscles and activated the Probe.

Tu Do died instantly, perhaps of the poison, perhaps of shock, it didn't much matter.

The Major withdrew the Probe, and, by means of a reverse plié, got off Tu Do. She checked his pulse, closed his eyelids, and took a long look at him. The man was very dead. His penis, however, still seemed alive, rigidly perpendicular to his prone, limp body, a tiny pinprick on the tip, with no sign of the expected post-mortem flaccidity.

"Fun's over, mister," said the Major, and extracted the body bag from beneath the altar.

After some rolling around, she was able to encase Tu Do in the plastic sack, but was prevented from zipping it up by his still-naggingly-insistent member.

She went to the altar, took out some gaffer's tape from her rucksack, and sat down next to him on the rug. Before she set about taping his organ to his stomach, she wrote out a little card which she tied to his big toe. It read: "#1. Foxy Fire Op. 2/7/68. VC."

She had no thoughts of sadness for the mortality of this man, only for her own cowardice on the sexual battlefield. Perhaps, she considered as she struggled against the iron strength of his manhood, she ought to recommend herself for court-martial when they returned to the States. It was, after all, the correct thing to do.

She had failed. Under fire, she had turned tail. She had killed the man, it was true, but in a violent, masculine way, like a frat brother who takes advantage of a passed-out coed. At the moment of truth she had been unable to staunch the bleeding of her female emotions. Though the L.P.A.R.D. made her body invulnerable, her mind refused to believe it. And Revelation was a hollow victory.

Tu Do's penis would not stay taped. Against all odds for her it kept popping up and pointing at her accusingly. The Major began to crack. Her hands shook, her lips trembled, and tears fell from her great, round eyes.

With terrible grief, she zipped up the body bag as far as she could, and took a Valium. In the morning, she would decide what to do.

In a drugged haze, Major Lincoln-Pruitt awoke to the sounds of jungle birds and female voices. It was dawn. Through the doorway, she could see the morning mist floating about the huge, green leaves, like edgeless clouds of angel hair. Over the speaker in the corner came the mingled chatterings of many happy women, excited, bright-toned chirpings that she could not make out specifically, but which cackled at her of success. No tears. Thank God.

She pulled herself up on her elbows and began to wake. She took a chance, and glanced over at the plastic-wrapped body of Tu Do. Through the opacity of the giant baggie, his features looked unformed, embryonic, like a prematurely-aborted pod person. Her eyes left his face and traveled hesitantly down his length.

"Jesus fucking Christ, I don't believe it!" The fireburst of her reaction exploded the sleep-fog in her brain, and she sat up wide awake.

"I don't fucking believe it. What is it—rigor mortis, now? What is this—the male furies they never told us about? Jesus!"

She was referring, of course, to Tu Do's penis, which, it seemed, against all biological reality, was still saluting. She buried her head in her hands, and engaged herself in conversation.

"Okay. Is this a symbol, or is it rhino horn? What's the story here, Major? You killed the slope but you couldn't kill his dick? Is this a joke? One of God's practical jokes? It is. It's a joke."

The Major started to laugh, nervously at first, uncertain of where it would lead her, then wildly and raucously, until she was flopping around the flokati like a big fish on a small hook. She might never have stopped but for a voice which, like a falling star in a clear night sky, plummeted out of the corner speaker and struck her mute. It spoke in Vietnamese, it was male, and the depth of emotion in it, as well as its dreadful significance, made her body temperature drop ten degrees. "I love you," Le Van Dong was saying tenderly to Mandy. "I love you."

The Major careened out the doorway and stood, tottering, in the morning mist. Her hut was at the apex of the semicircle, and everywhere she looked in both directions, she could see a steady stream of Vietnamese men emerging from the other huts.

Wavering gently, with gimlet eyes and smiles of surfeit, the men wafted by her in the wispy dew, unseeing, lost in hope, like a parade of zombies unexpectedly blessed. The women of the platoon lounged at their doorways, lilting their slender arms and hands in gestures of farewell, their sleepy voices nestling on the bed of fog. "See you tonight, darling . . . goodbye, sweetie . . . till tonight then."

Major Lincoln-Pruitt flattened herself against the doorway of her hootch. The men must not see the dead one. For a full half hour of morning-after leavetaking, the Major was stretched across her entrance like a human condom. By the time the last man was gone, she was, quite literally, stiff with rage.

Two minutes later, a one-woman mortar barrage, she was in front of the pagoda surrounded by her troops.

"What the hell happened here?" she screamed, Edith Piaf on the rampage. "What is the meaning of this mutiny? Rasmussen?"

"I fell in love," said Mandy, shrugging her birdlike shoulders, a look of pure bliss cuddling her dreamy eyes. "I never thought it was possible. I hate men. I do, honestly. But Le's different. He's asked me to marry him. I think I'm going to settle down here in An Hui."

"Great." The Major was seething now, her tongue and lips

barely able to form vowels. "You must have got the guy I wanted. Smith?"

Fantasy stood with her hands on her hips, absolutely furious. "He had herpes. Can you believe that? There we are just about to do it, everything's really nice, and then I happened to look down, thank God, and I saw it. 'God, man,' I said to this guy, 'thanks a lot. You've got herpes and you were just going to do it without telling me and I'd have it for life. That's really honorable, thanks. Some Asian. Anyway, he was really embarrassed and everything, and he says he's had it for a week and it's almost gone and he thought it was all right to take the chance but I was probably right to wait one more day. He's shooting me a tiger and giving me the skins tonight to make up for it. You know, Major, herpes is incurable."

"I know. I know. Jackson?" The Major sounded weary.

Zinnia stood at attention and said tonelessly, "My weapon jammed, ma'am. I activated the Probe and nothing happened." She dropped her eyes and went on to admit, "I could not have used the Shredder or the Laser and lived with myself. I'm working on the mechanism now, Major."

"A problem I had not foreseen. Interesting. All right, Jackson. And you, Dinah, even you?" The Major's words were cracked and bruised.

Dinah's Welsh being quivered with denial. "He couldn't get it up. I tried everything. He's into S.&M., you know? Well, I tried my whole repertoire. I'm exhausted. I'm sorry, Major. I'm the best dominatrix there is. How do you think I feel?"

"Damn!" The Major spat out. "The Army will simply have to budget for aphrodisiacs. It's a battle I had with them from the beginning. Men cannot be counted on to get an erection every time. Even if they have every intention of getting one they often don't. But tell me, Dinah, how do I convince the Joint Chiefs of that?"

"I see your point, ma'am. Major?" Dinah hung her head. "I have a confession to make."

The Major waited.

"For the last week every day I've put a little Spanish fly in the food. I thought it would make us gung-ho. In spite of our other problems I think it did."

The Major looked worried.

"In my food? You put Spanish fly in my food?"

"No, Major," Dinah quickly assured her, "never in your food. I . . ."

"Why not in my food, Dinah?" The Major was livid. "Do I look like the kind of woman who could have sex with just any guy out of the jungle with complete poise and relaxation? I'm not a slut, you know, Dinah."

Dinah's eyes pleaded for forgiveness. "You want some now?" she asked timidly.

"It's too late now," replied the Major. "So what the hell happened with your girls?"

Dinah buried her head in her hands. Carol Mayhew, Canadian prostate expert, stepped forward representing the fifteen women in Dinah's stable. "The truth is, Major, we never really understood what you meant by pubococcyneal muscles. I mean, we thought we did, but when push came to shove, none of us could operate the L.P.A.R.D."

"But you're prostitutes! You have sex for a living! Don't you ever fake orgasm?" The Major was flabbergasted.

Carol's cheeks reddened with embarrassment. "No," she confessed. "We might say we do, but the truth is we don't have orgasms at all, even fake ones. We don't know how."

"But what about the training? There was a muscle chart and exercises designed specially by Lotte Berk in London."

"The muscle chart reminded me of once when I went to a gynecologist to get fitted for a diaphragm. He showed me this three-dimensional pelvic sculpture and started explaining where the diaphragm fits. And I said, 'Hold it. When I put my hand in there all I can feel is dark and damp and some strange ridges. What it may look like has nothing to do with the way it

feels.' As for the exercises, they were so difficult. We haven't
exercised since we were kids. We're known for our soft,
squishy cuddlyness around Manhattan. If you want your bony
models you don't come to Dinah's."

The Major sighed. "Jackson, after the briefing, come to my
hootch and I will give you an instrument known as a vibrator.
I got it in Japan, but someday, American women will be buying
them like Tupperware. It's an orgasmic aid. Make sure that by
nightfall, each of Dinah's girls knows, in the Biblical sense,
what we mean by pubococcyneal muscles."

"Gee," said Carol, turning to the others, "I think I've always
been afraid if I come I might die." She stepped back into the
ranks.

"*La petite morte*, Carol. We all feel that way at first. You'll
get used to it. Now. It may interest you ladies to know that
last night I made my kill." The women gasped. "He now lies
within my hootch, in view of circumstances, a grisly anachro-
nism. What, my foxes, is wrong with this picture?" The women
looked at each other but kept mute. "Well, when the enemy
discovers that one of their own is missing, they will be right
back here demanding an explanation of what has happened
to their comrade. There will be interrogation, perhaps shooting
or nastiness with knives." The women moaned in concert. A
ripple of fear passed over them. "And what will we tell them?
Rasmussen, what will we tell them?"

"I don't know," muttered Mandy.

"You will tell them that the man and I have run away together. That you are shocked and horrified by such wanton
behavior from a nun, but what with the war and the American
influence, it's hardly surprising. Is it?"

"Will you really leave, then?" asked Dinah.

"I have no choice, Wentworth. He must be buried. Or in this
heat he will turn and, like a Judas, give us all away. I am
going upriver to get rid of the evidence. In the meantime,
Jackson, you will be in charge. Use the daylight hours to plant

the kitchen gardens. I want those seedlings coming up when I get back, which should be in the early hours of tomorrow morning.

"Now, Wentworth." Dinah snapped to attention. "Go to my hootch, get on the radio, and summon the Pimp Cav for dawn tomorrow. Anyone who is not escorted by a bounteous body bag, at that time, will be left behind on this LZ to explain to the wives of An Hui our mysterious disappearance. A fate I, from my knowledge of Vietnamese women, would not wish even on a Marine." Dinah scurried off to the Major's hootch. "Tonight, Jackson will give the signal and you will effect penetration and activate the Probe. The former last night convinced me you can do, the latter, let me say from experience, is but one more turn of the screw. Get to work! Rasmussen! Smith! Find the wheelbarrow and bring it to my hut. Jackson, come with me. Dismissed!"

The Major stormed off through the hearth doorway into her hut. Dinah was just finishing the transmission, her eyes glued to the marbleized lingam of Tu Do.

"You see this?" The Major flicked her finger against the rock-hard monument and caused it to sway like a metronome. Dinah nodded. "Rhino horn. Here." The Major removed a tiny packet from beneath her watch. "Take it. Pour it in his drink. As you can see"—she flicked it again—"it works." She gazed up at the giant black woman. "As of this moment, Jackson, you are in command. As soon as I have disposed of him, I'll be back." The Major, softened by her own failure, was forgiving. "If I don't make it in time, give the signal for me. See that we take the hill."

"I promise," said Jackson. "You can count on me."

"I can count," said the Major, "only on rhino horn. Bring me my lip gloss."

Dinah trotted to the altar, retrieved the little jar, and gave it to the Major. Mandy and Fantasy arrived at the forest doorway, dragging the wheelbarrow behind them. They maneuvered it into the hut, saw Tu Do, and looked at each other in amazement.

"What on earth is that?" said Fantasy.

"That," replied the Major, gesturing at the obelisk, "that, young ladies, is the persistence of myth. Let's move out."

The four junior officers lifted Tu Do onto the wagon and pushed it through the door. The Major took hold of the handles and strode into the forest, pushing her quarry before her.

Le Van Dong stood in the meeting house before a gaggle of hysterical, female hamlet-dwellers. Behind him, using him for a shield, the invasion force, those men who had made contact with the nuns, were assembled in a lineup. "They are," Le was saying, "a group of refugee Buddhist nuns from Nepal, driven out by the Chinese Communists."

"They don't look Nepalese," shouted Ho Chi Minh's wife sullenly.

"There are many minorities in Asia who do not look Asian," replied Le. "Are we now to be slaves to our own negative stereotype?" The men behind him cheered at his logic.

"What the Tao were you doing all night? Ho Chi Binh hasn't looked this good since before I married him. He still had hair then." Ho Chi Binh's wife led the other women in a blast of jeers.

"We were gathering information. Did you know, for example, that, in Nepal, the leopard is sacred rather than the tiger?"

"Who cares?" hooted the women.

"Well, the Cult Committee cares," said Le, gesturing toward Tran Van Luc. "But be that as it may, you'll be relieved to know that we found the nuns extremely cooperative and no threat to the safety of An Hui." The men nodded enthusiastically.

"What about the helicopters?" yelled one woman.

"They say they came on foot, and that the American planes happened by just as they arrived. A coincidence. I remind you, nobody saw the choppers land."

"A coincidence, eh?" Ho Chi Binh's wife was not placated. "It's a long haul from Nepal."

"Yes," agreed Le, "and it's a long haul from North Vietnam. If you no longer trust my judgment, let me now step down as cadre leader."

Howls of "No, no," "We didn't mean it," and such filled the meeting house, and Le resumed speaking.

"They are only camping for a week, after which time they will move on. Tonight, and every night until they leave, I and the other men will stand guard around the LZ. It is best that you women stay away from there, just in case there's any trouble.

"Guarding the LZ is thankless and exhausting work, but we are doing it for you. The most important thing to us individually, and to the Party as a whole, is that the women of An Hui be kept safe."

The women cheered and embraced their husbands as heroes. Le made his way through the crowd and left the building. Much was troubling him.

For one thing, Ao Dai was nowhere to be found. Probably she was angry with him over the pig incident, and then his callousness about her lunar cycle. He hoped she had not seen him with the nun. For if he were to tell himself the truth, last night he had forgotten all he had ever learned in his reeducation classes. He had, quite simply, fallen head over tire treads in love. With Mandeh. From where? A Buddhist nun from what sect? He did not know.

What he had told the women of An Hui he had pieced together from scraps of knowledge dimly recalled by the other men. En masse, they had learned nothing, nothing logical, rational, or concrete. And he, well, from the moment he saw Mandeh, his intelligence seemed to drop from his brain to his loins, where it had uncaringly resided until dawn.

Tonight, he resolved. Tonight he would interrogate her. He would pin her eggshell limbs to the furry rug and prevent her escape with the weight of his body. He would stare into her sea-blue eyes and, threatening her with his manliness, force her to tell him of her mission. Tonight he would ask the cold, clear questions that last night, for some wonderful, unknown reason, he had been unable to ask. It was going to be all right. The smell of Mandeh's perfume lingered on his body, and convinced him all was safe.

He was thankful that Ao Dai, with her insightful mind, had not been at the meeting. Her absence concerned him, but he chalked it up to female jealousy, and, in the afterglow of love, soon forgot about her.

It is a sad, but not surprising, commentary on the hamlet of An Hui, that not a soul out of its seventy inhabitants ever noticed that Tu Do was missing.

Ao Dai staggered through the tangled forest like one possessed. Once again she had escaped, not unscathed, never unscathed, but she was still alive with all her limbs, and in a war such as this, that was all anyone could ask.

The Marines had been curiously lethargic with her, more respectful than usual, as if, for a change, they recognized her humanity and suspected her of having morals. They had raped her not indifferently, but almost nostalgically, as if somehow she were lost to them as an enemy. Her escape had been easy. They didn't seem to care. It was very strange.

Upon escaping, she had run for the network of tunnels near the LZ. She had hid there, underground, for hours, awaiting the inevitable, but it never came. At dawn, she emerged, and the Marines had vanished, as mysteriously as they had appeared, leaving no carnage behind them. From a tree in the forest she had watched in surprise as Le and the other men departed the huts and returned via the footpath to An Hui. She did not know what was happening. It was all very strange. Later, though she dreaded it, she would have to talk to Le.

She still had her rifle. That was strange too. The Marines

had left it lying easily within her reach, as if, when she ran, they wanted her to have a weapon against them, as if it was only fair. She used it now, bayonetting the tangled foliage, fighting her way to the river.

Major Lincoln-Pruitt was struggling with Tu Do. Using a sickle forgotten by one of the men, she had spent hours hacking at the underbrush, clearing a path to the river. She had pulled and pushed the wheelbarrow over tree stumps and through matted vines, and now that she had reached her goal, she had no energy left. She was too tired to lift him, and so, instead, she sat down by the edge of the water, leaned against a rock, and rested. Soon it would be dusk.

It was lovely there by the Oma River, hot and cool depending on the wind currents, blissfully quiet except for a background hum of invisible forest creatures who fluttered and scurried, this way and that, foraging for their nests. Around Tu Do, a party of flies buzzed with merriment, and, because he was beginning to smell, the Major roused herself and pushed him a yard or two back from the riverbank and into the forest. She was not yet ready for his funeral. She wanted to cleanse herself first.

The sun, in its decline, shot its rays like deadbolts through the open water, and portions of the bank were bathed in the most golden and secret of lights. Into one of these sun zones now stepped the Major, stark naked, filthy with sweat and oil, and clutching, in her tiny hand, her saffron robes which she intended to wash.

She shut her eyes against the glare and waded into the river. The water came up to her thighs, and she bent down and spread her saffron robes out on the surface. She watched distractedly as the orange gauze billowed with air bubbles and eddied in a gentle circle, and when it began to sink, she took it up, squeezed it out, and used it for a washcloth.

Carefully, she spread her legs, and began to wash away the

grime of battle. She was sore. The ferocity of her attack had exposed her womanly parts for the raw recruits they truly were. She moaned softly as the cool water met her chafed surfaces, and wondered casually if this was how it felt to have been raped.

Another moan, not hers, caused her to open her eyes and see, not five yards down the bank, in exactly the same state of nudity, in the same position in the water, and actually doing the self-same ablutions, a young and rather grimy Vietnamese woman.

"How odd," the Major said in Vietnamese. "It's like a mirror image."

"You!" said Ao Dai in disbelief. "You." And then, curiously, "Were you raped?"

"In a manner of speaking." The Major glanced behind her to make sure that Tu Do remained hidden. And then, noting the whereabouts of her sickle, asked, "Were you?"

"You know I was," said Ao Dai, and she wrung out her black pajamas and disappeared onto the riverbank.

The Major finished washing and put back on her saffron robes. She took up her sickle and waited.

Still the only noise was that of the forest's inhabitants, but the stench from Tu Do was potent now, almost overwhelming. She longed for the privacy to have done with him.

The sharp nose of a bayonet poked at her shoulder, and, slowly, she turned, inwardly praising the Vietnamese woman for her mastery of stealth. She held the sickle tautly in her deceptively childlike hand.

Ao Dai, wet and half-washed, her pigtails dripping, trained her M16 rifle on the Major's throat. First she would get the information. Then she would drag this woman to Le and prove to him, once and for all, that she had been right, that a clear mind, even in the body of a female, had no sex. She looked down at the sickle in the woman's hand. The fact that she recognized it as belonging to Tran Van Luc, brought back the anguish of the night before and further incensed her. Perhaps killing this slut would be a better victory.

"You," Ao Dai spoke through clenched teeth. "It is you who have spun this web to lure our men. You, who lulled them into forgetfulness and immorality! I know your game: With your flesh, you gentle them to boyhood and then, like a lazy lady mantis, you summon your Marines to bite off their heads and finish the kill. How weak! How spineless!"

"Never!" The full well of the Major's pride boiled over within her, and the word spat out of her mouth with shocking intensity.

"Never would I shill for the Marines! Though my finger and toe nails be ripped from my body! Though my nipples be smeared with honey as bait for bears! The Marines—hah! No delicacy! No flair! No sensitivity in the kill! Do you think I have spent my life only to be some bimbo adjutant on the arm of grunts and slime? I had a higher opinion of the Vietnamese woman's mind. I see I was mistaken."

Ao Dai, confused by this outburst, and, by a gust of wind, inundated with the stench of decay, maneuvered herself and her captive into the forest and found Tu Do. His fat, squat body had swollen with death, and now pushed tensely against its plastic casing. His penis, still standing, open to the heat and humidity, was laden with flies, and both women gasped in disgust.

"Oh my gods," said Ao Dai. "Tu Do. Tu Do. What an end."

"A just end," the Major said coldly, "judging by his personality."

Ao Dai prodded her captive away from the corpse and back to the riverbank. The two women were silent for a moment as they both took deep breaths of clean air. Then with grim determination, Ao Dai spoke.

"How did you kill him? What is your weapon?" She shoved the bayonet between the Major's collarbones. "What is your weapon?"

The Major smiled and said nothing.

Demanding now, forgetting Le, the hamlet, her rape, and her Communism in the frenzy of her discovery, Ao Dai pressed on.

"It's inside you, isn't it? It's inside you!"

The sun was descending, now, behind the trees, and Ao Dai pushed the Major into the last remaining shaft of light.

"How brilliant," she said, her slope eyes wide with excitement. "Why didn't I think of it myself? It's so obvious. I've been raped so many times, by so many Marines. Why, if I'd had this weapon, there'd be no Green Berets left or ARVN! Give me that weapon! Give it to me or I'll rip your throat out and take it!"

"Never!" The Major raised her sickle. "You'll never get it, you're too stupid. Submissive, like all Asian women, and groveling. 'Let me get your shoes, master, your tea'—revolting! You may be a woman, geisha brain, but you're a Viet Cong too, and, as such, my enemy!"

"How dare you call me 'geisha brain'—you with your Marine grunts for backup! Oh, yes, you'd like me to believe you are on your own—superwomen—no men allowed. But I saw your grunts! I saw them checking on you, watching out for you in case of trouble, annoyed and petulant with the men you lured, like fathers with their daughters' first dates. Pathetic! Like all Western women—sucking on Daddy's hind tit! And they raped me, your Marine swine, and if I'd only had that weapon—"

"What?" The Major shrieked with rage and realization. "Where? When? How long ago?"

Ao Dai could not answer, for at that moment a force greater than any woman's fury suddenly shocked the earth. A terrible concussion, a rain of mortar burst, shellfire, and bomb blast cracked the now-dark sky over LZ My Sinh. The two women were knocked to the ground, and lay there stunned as the distant heavens blazed with pink and red lightning. The noise was that of a volcano exploding, and the women held their hands to their ears and their knees to their chests, and wept for the peace of the womb.

Tu Do's body was propelled from the wagon and sailed by them, like an errant spirit of the forest on some Dionysian quest. Where he came to rest, they never knew, for now they leapt up and both began to run, toward the horror, toward the death knell, fearless and driven like women in love.

Five hours later, false dawn broke over LZ My Sinh and revealed in its phony light a hell on earth. A fog of smoke and mist snaked along the shattered remains of Firebase Fox, splintered here and there by the reddish glow of lava lamps miraculously missed.

Into this nightmare of what might have been staggered the exhausted figures of Ao Dai and the Major, their clothes torn and ragged, their skin scraped and bloody, their ears ringing with thunder.

Death was everywhere, as shrewish as an open mouth, as modest as a dismembered foot. The Major stumbled through the rubble of her dreams, searching for a clue, a holy grail, an answer. Like a living fish in a sea of blood, she navigated these grisly depths, this cluttered ocean of femininity. Petticoats and padded bras, powder puffs and perfume bottles, slender limbs and torsos in repose, stiletto-heeled boots that still contained the feet but nothing else. A heap of stuffed animals covered with blood, some autograph hounds of hell. A human-hair purse. *Guernica* in pink. And then she noticed something: little cards tied to toes. Toes on feet, toes alone, male toes on male bodies—everywhere.

Like a rat in a sewer, she ran to and fro, back and forth, gathering, gathering, taking the little cards and counting, counting. Nineteen! There were nineteen in all. "Look!" she cried to Ao Dai across the fire and waste. "Look!" She held out the little cards for her to see. "You see! The men were already dead. When the air strike hit, the men were already dead! Victory!"

Ao Dai stood amidst the feminine debris. Near her feet, the head of Le Van Dong lolled in death. She looked down at it, and with the full force of her female being, kicked it into the trees. The roar of an approaching chopper shocked her to attention, and she screamed at the Major, "Run! Run!" and streaked off the LZ and made for the tunnels.

The Major stood her ground. Hands on her hips, her eyes black with fury, she glowered at the descending chopper. Then, spying a Kalashnikov rifle beneath a tangle of nylons, she seized it, dropped to one knee, and aimed it at the cockpit.

"Far out, man," Hayes was saying. "Look at all those heads. Looks like a fucking pool table down there, Tommy." He popped a cassette into the tape player and the Rolling Stones flooded the cockpit.

"Jesus!" Davis dipped the chopper and banked low so they could see better. "Sure as hell does, Larry. What a mess. The headless horsewomen, hey, Larry? They really gonna call this a friendly-fire casualty?"

"Sure." Hayes held his breath and passed the joint. "Why not? Who's to know different?" He breathed out and the sweet smoke swirled around the cockpit.

"Clever," said Davis, sucking on the joint. "Very clever. Sometimes you got to hand it to those grunts, you—hey! Down! Get down, man! Get down!" Davis grabbed the joystick as hard as he could and the aircraft zoomed skyward. "Bitch!" he muttered as he leveled off. "Did you see her, Larry? Of all the fucking nerve! Cong-fucker!"

"I'm hit, Tom." Hayes was holding his shoulder and whining. "She got me."

Davis looked at Hayes for a moment and then handed him the joint. He circled the LZ and prepared to fire.

"You lucky shit," he said as he went in for the kill. "You'll get a Purple Heart." The first bullets spat up cones of debris as they hit earth. He fired again. "At least a month dicking off in Saigon." The Major was running for cover but tripped on a copy of the *I Ching*. "All the smack you can shoot." The next volley ripped through her back and pinned her to the LZ. "And all the broads you can prong. Some people," he said as he fired once more at her tiny frame and then began his ascent, "have all the luck." He hovered for a moment and leaned out the cockpit window.

"Make love not war, sweetheart," he called, and waved to her as he banked the ship, and sped off to Fire Support Base 218, home of Avenger Corps, which had just dug in about a mile and a half to the south.

As soon as the chopper had gone, Ao Dai surfaced on the LZ and ran to the Major. She turned her over and covered her with one of the flokati rugs. The Major was gasping, trying to speak. Ao Dai bent her head and put her ear next to the Major's lips.

"What is it?" she said. "What are you saying?"

The Major's words were barely audible, but finally she managed to be heard. "What size diaphragm do you wear?" she wheezed.

Ao Dai was taken aback. "Oh," she said, thinking furiously, trying to remember that one visit to the French clinic so long ago. "Oh, um, uh, sixty-five? Yes, that's it! Sixty-five!"

"Perfect," the Major sputtered. "Me too." With one final crushing effort, the Major then pushed away the rug, reached down between her legs, and extracted the L.P.A.R.D. She cleaned it on the rug and thrust it at Ao Dai.

"Here," she whispered. "Take it. I won't be needing it anymore." Ao Dai took it and began to weep. A deep, life-stealing shudder throttled the Major's little body, and her eyelids slowly shut. "Oil it first," was the last thing she said before she died.

· ·

Some months later, during the May Offensive, Avenger Corps invaded the Au Shau Valley. While tromping through the high grass, the Advance Recon Patrol came upon a party of Vietnamese women, semi-nude, and bathing in an abandoned paddy. The spokeswoman for the group stepped forward. She was small but sturdy, with black pigtails, and she wore only the top of her black pajamas and was naked from the waist down. Her slope eyes rounded with fear, and she covered her private parts nervously as she spoke.

"Please don't rape us," she said in broken English. "Please, not rape. Anything but rape."

The grunts looked at each other and leered. Suddenly, they broke ranks, and, with arms outstretched, lunged toward the helpless females. Terrified, the women bolted and, each in a different direction, ran for their lives into the high grass.

The spokeswoman ran east. Her little feet pounded through the valley at top speed, and, twice, she glanced backwards as she fled, measuring the distance between her and her pursuer. When she was sure she had run far enough, she began to slow down. Ao Dai grinned as she heard the grunt catching up with her.

Wrinkled Linen

It was one of those days when they were fighting. After the news, they fought about where to eat dinner and he suggested the Russian Tea Room.

"I don't want to eat there," she said. "We have to get dressed up if we eat there and it's all the way uptown. Every time I go there I'm reminded of Christmas."

"That's why I like it," he said.

In the taxi going uptown, he noticed that she was wearing the pin he had given her for Christmas. She noticed that he had put on the birthday tie. This show of respect for each other's taste caused a momentary truce and they both leaned back against the leather Checker seats and decided to relax. They were friendly but silent until they reached the Port Authority Bus Terminal.

"God," she said, rolling her eyeballs heavenward, "I'm sorry, but I cannot believe how many homeless people are living on the streets of New York City. It's like Calcutta. Only in Calcutta it's families, in New York it's singles. Typical."

"Yeah," he said. "There's a couple of old guys who live in front of the Greenwich Theatre. They hit me up for money every time I go by there."

"And you always give it to them, don't you?" He nodded. "I don't know why you're so big on giving derelicts money. What is it, luck? There but for the grace of God?"

"I'm a nice guy," he said.

"You are a nice guy. No one's disputing that. I guess that makes me a lucky gal, doesn't it?"

"Yes," he said, smiling, "yes it does. You're a very lucky gal."

"I used to have a girlfriend who always gave money to bums when she was between boyfriends and looking. She thought it would bring her luck in finding a fabulous guy."

"Did it?" he asked.

"I don't know," she replied. "She's married to a guy now but she isn't always happy."

He said nothing. There was a silence as they both stared out the windows. She spoke first.

"What are you thinking?" she said.

"I'm thinking about dinner and what I'm going to eat. I'm hungry."

She nodded wearily. "Okay," she sighed. "Okay."

"What?" he asked.

"Nothing, nothing. I just thought maybe you might be thinking about that last thing I said."

"What?" he asked again.

"The thing about my friend who sometimes isn't happy and I thought you might be thinking, 'Like us,' because sometimes we fight."

"No," he said.

"No, what?" she asked.

"No, I wasn't thinking about that. I was thinking about dinner and what to order."

"Great," she said, sighing again. "Great. Okay, so what are you having?"

"I don't know," he said.

"Look," she said, staring him in the eye, "my parents didn't pay thousands of dollars for a fancy education for me to have conversations like this. I'm a verbal person. It said so on my kindergarten report. I must have discussions with others on topics of weight. How can I live with someone who never talks to me? It's like being in a Japanese hotbox in solitary confinement. I feel like my brain is starving to death for lack of human contact. The thing about Man is his power of speech. Do you understand wherefrom I'm coming, Mr. No Mincing of Words?"

He looked petulant. "We talk," he said.

The cab pulled up in front of the Russian Tea Room and she got out, slamming the door behind her. She went through the revolving door and spoke to the maître d'. When he came in, he joined her standing on the line.

"I just don't see what good it is having a successful boyfriend if he never talks to me," she said.

"1 can't just talk when you say talk. I'm spontaneous. And when you tell me to talk I clam up and it takes me some time to recover."

"Can you talk now?" she asked.

"Not yet," he answered and turned away.

"When? Soon?" she asked hopefully.

"Maybe," he replied.

"Oh, look," she exclaimed, quite excited, "there's Sylvia Sidney!"

"Who?" he asked.

"Forget it," she answered and kept silent until the maître d' led them to the table.

He ordered the hot borscht and beef Stroganoff. She ordered the chicken Kiev and the hot borscht. He would eat half of his piroshki. She would eat hers and the other half of his. He ordered a vodka gimlet and also ordered a bottle of wine for them to share.

"Now don't drink too much just because we're having a fight and you think you ought to drown your sorrows," she said.

He gave her a sarcastic smile and took a big gulp of his drink.

"Okay, I get it, fuck you, Mom," she said and didn't say another thing until the food came.

They were seated at one of the side tables for two, closed in on either side by other tables, excruciatingly close to their neighbors. The tablecloths were pink, as was the lighting, and Christmas balls and tinsel were in profusion even though it was summer. The decor had not changed in her entire life.

"You know," she said, trying to start anew, "I ate chicken Kiev here before I went to the first Beatles concert ever held in America, at Carnegie Hall in 1964. I had just finished eleventh grade.

"They were wearing sharkskin suits with velveteen lapels. Happy Rockefeller was in the first row and walked out in the middle, taking her kids with her. It was an event. To my knowledge there had never been a rock concert before. We screamed and got very excited. My friend DeeDee got us into the press conference after and we met them. Ringo said to me, 'Don't we know you?' DeeDee had her picture taken with John. It was in the yearbook."

"It must have been great," he said.

"Yeah," she said. "The sixties. I adored the sixties. All my dreams came true in the sixties. I was blissfully happy. In the seventies, I had to recover from all that happiness. In the eighties, I'm finally a real person."

He laughed. She continued.

"Something happened today that's made me understand the eighties: I was shopping and I came across these fabulous beige linen jodhpurs which I bought right away. I had vowed never to wear jodhpurs after seeing Elizabeth Taylor from behind in *Reflections in a Golden Eye*. But they look okay. They look good; I'm like a mini Ronald Reagan. Anyhow, linen is a classy material, really fine, and it was 'in' when I was in high school too. We had linen dresses, and when you wore them, your whole life was about keeping them pressed and starched. Linen wrinkles like a motherfucker, but here's the thing, it was really low and slutty and ill-bred if you wore a linen dress with a wrinkle in it. I remember never sitting down, never raising my arms, and still always having wrinkles. So, today, I'm trying on these jodhpurs and I glance at the label and what do you think it says? 'Guaranteed to Wrinkle.' And I realized that's what the eighties is all about: off-color coordinates. What do the eighties mean to you, Mr. Snuggles?"

She smiled at him and went back to eating. He thought for a while and then said, "The most freedom anyone's ever had while teetering on the edge of disaster."

"On the edge of disaster? What do you mean by that?"

"Well, any minute the world could blow up," he explained.

"Yeah? . . . Yeah?" She waited. "Say more."

He shrugged. "No more. Want to see a movie after dinner?"

She seemed exasperated. "I love the way you hasten from the cosmic to the particular. It keeps me on my toes. We could. We could see a movie, only . . ."

"Only what?"

"Only it's such an isolating experience seeing a movie: people sitting in a darkened room staring at a screen. I thought we could go home, have sex, and talk about life."

He nodded. "We could do both," he said.

"Both?" she repeated. "Oh. All right. Let me think about it. I'll tell you at the end of the dinner. I can't think about it in this light. All I can think about are nutcrackers and sugar-plums."

"And, oh, Father Christmas, if you love me at all, please bring me a big red India-rubber ball," he recited suddenly.

"What a wonderful poem that is. Do you remember the picture of King John?"

"A scrawny guy with an effete look on his face."

"His crime was that he wouldn't share his toys?"

"I think so."

"It's funny what we have in common," she said, smiling. "We both ate out of identical baby dishes and our favorite Golden Book was *The Tawny Scrawny Lion*."

"And we're young, we're American, and we like comedy," he added.

"Is it enough, do you think?" she asked with mock concern.

"Depends," he replied.

"Well, I don't know, sometimes it worries me. Like the time I was reading the biography of Jean-Paul Sartre and Simone de Beauvoir, and I looked up from the book and told you how Sartre and de Beauvoir had lived together for fifty years in the same hotel but on different floors. And you replied . . ."

He didn't remember.

"Goddam faggots! And I had to explain, of course, how not only were they not homosexual, they weren't both men."

"Well, it's true," he said, refilling their wineglasses, "I don't read as much as I should."

"How can you not read? I don't get it."

"I should read more," he said.

"Okay, look." She rubbed her eyes with her hand. "I know I'm a reactionary asshole who lives in the past. I know people don't read so much and it's the modern world: TV, computers, designer jeans. You can give your body to science when you renew your driver's license now. You just fill out the enclosed coupon and when they scoop you up off the Long Island Expressway, they take you right to the organ bank. But I don't feel comfortable with it in the least. When I was growing up, 'fast' was a dirty word, fast girls, fast and loose. Now it's the wave of the future: fast food, fast forward. Last week, they redefined 'catastrophe.' I saw it on the news. Used to be a catastrophe indicated a million dollars damage. Now it's five million."

"That's inflation for you," he said.

"But that's all you feel about it?" she asked. "Don't you ever feel a lack? Don't you ever long for some quiet excellence?"

"Like what?" he asked.

"Well, sometimes I wish I was wearing a long skirt with tons of petticoats and a corset that restricted my movements. I wish that what we were doing tonight was sitting in our living room by candlelight and that you were reading aloud to me, and after we'd play classical music together. I wish there were no television, no radio, no stereo, no telephone . . ."

"No polio vaccines, no diaphragms," he helped.

"I don't have the nerves for it," she said. "Modern life worries me. It's too fast. I worry about it all the time. Why don't you ever worry? I know: because you're younger. Because you're twenty-eight and I'm thirty-three. When you're thirty, you'll worry."

"It never changes things to worry about them. And you are a modern girl; you just refuse to think of yourself that way."

"I guess." She sighed. "Isn't there any other time you wish you'd lived in?"

"The future," he said without hesitation. "After the blast."

"It might be kind of weird then, mightn't it? You'd have a genetic mutant for a mistress, probably just as nervous as me but with three eyes and no nose."

"We'd hunt together." He smiled. "Giant pheasants. We'd fish for walleye the size of sharks."

"Where's this, upstate New York?"

"Yeah. That's where I'd want to be after the blast: up near the boundary waters."

"Once a lakedweller always a lakedweller. If I'm still alive, could I come with you?"

"Maybe," he said.

"Maybe? Well, maybe I wouldn't want to. Thanks. Now I feel bad."

"Why?" he asked, summoning the waiter to order dessert.

"Because you don't want me with you after the blast."

"I didn't say that," he said.

"But you meant it," she replied and they ordered dessert. They both had the boysenberry jello and coffee. He also had a Courvoisier and asked for the check. Sylvia Sidney left the restaurant and Sylvia Miles entered and was given the same table. He drank the last of the wine and noticed none of the comings and goings.

"Want to see a movie?" he asked again.

"I don't know," she answered mournfully.

"Well, we could get a paper and see what's playing." She said nothing. He waited. She cried a little into her napkin, not looking at him. He sipped his Courvoisier and noticed Johnny Bench sitting at the back of the restaurant. Finally, she spoke.

"No, I don't want to see a movie," she said passionately, "I want to make human contact with another person. Most of the time you're at work and then once in a while, we get these snatches of time and you always want to see a movie. Maybe you could watch me for ninety minutes for a change. You could eat popcorn while you're doing it so it wouldn't be so boring." She wiped away her tears with the pink napkin.

"All right," he said, "we won't see a movie."

"No," she said definitely. "See a movie. Don't let me stand in your way of seeing a movie. I don't mean to cause a scene. It's just . . . I'm thinking about what you said this afternoon and it really upset me."

"What?" he asked, curious.

"The thing about emotional pain not being as bad as physical pain. I don't see how you can say that."

"Oh," he said, remembering. "Well, I feel sorrier for a guy who's been in a car accident than for a guy who's fucked up emotionally."

"But physical pain is finite and emotional pain is infinite."

"I don't agree."

"But surely the pain is less when you can see what's hurting?"

"For a guy with a gaping wound in his chest, it's no consolation."

"I can't believe you're saying this," she said, shaking her head sadly. "It's so cold, so brutally rational, like the drowning of unwanted kittens. It's a direct assault on everything I believe and hold sacred. I hope you realize that."

189 · *Wrinkled Linen*

The waiter arrived with the check. She continued. "What about people with awful childhoods? What about them?"

"They still have their own minds," he replied. "But a person who's blind will never see. A person who's deaf will never hear. That makes me sad."

"Are you saying emotional pain is a choice?" she asked, outraged.

"A kind of choice," he replied and extracted his wallet from his pocket and began to lay out money.

She sputtered with fury. "I cannot believe . . . It's like having a Nazi storm trooper for a boyfriend."

"You knew the job was dangerous when you took it," he said.

"She's right, you know." A resonant French-accented voice set sail from the table on their left and landed between them. They both looked its way, surprised, and came face to face with a very handsome Frenchman who was eating alone excruciatingly close to them. "Excuse me," the Frenchman said to them, "but I could not help overhearing. I believe she is right in what she says." The Frenchman addressed this last to him. "I can see that she is a very sensitive person and perhaps she is trying to tell you something that you are refusing to hear."

"What?" he asked. She listened with delight.

"Well," began the Frenchman, looking at her, "perhaps she is trying to say that she is fragile and that you have bruised her with your rationality and what she needs is a softer thing, understanding, compassion, sympathy."

"I think you're right," he said.

"Yes," she agreed.

"I'm glad we got that settled," he said, rising. "Shall we?" He inclined his head questioningly toward her. "Coming?" he asked unnecessarily.

"Oh, yes," she replied and pushed out the table. "Goodbye." She smiled at the Frenchman.

"I hope I have not interfered," the Frenchman said, gesturing with his hands, "but we were so close."

"Not at all," she said over her shoulder and proceeded on out to Fifty-seventh Street.

They walked to Sixth Avenue in silence and he bought a paper.

"Ten o'clock. The Bond movie. Forty-fourth and Broadway. Coming?" he said gruffly.

"I think he was right about my sensitivity and my fragility," she said, giggling. "And he was handsome too."

"Maybe you ought to get him to take you home, then. You could talk."

"Not necessarily," she said and took his arm. "Boy, are you grumpy."

"If you can't handle MiGs," he snapped, "don't fly in MiG Alley."

"I'll keep that in mind," she said and stood by as he hailed a taxi.

ABOUT THE AUTHOR

Emily Prager grew up in Texas, the Far East, and Greenwich Village. She was graduated from the Brearley School and Barnard College, where she majored in anthropology. She has been a contributing editor for *The National Lampoon* and *Viva*, and a political satirist for *Penthouse*; she currently writes humor and TV criticism for *The Village Voice*. She is the author of four books, three of which are fiction— *World War II Resistance Stories, A Visit from the Footbinder and Other Stories*, and *Clea & Zeus Divorce*.

VINTAGE
CONTEMPORARIES

"Today's novels for the readers of today." — VANITY FAIR

"Real literature—originals and important reprints—in attractive, inexpensive paperbacks." — THE LOS ANGELES TIMES

"Prestigious." — THE CHICAGO TRIBUNE

"A very fine collection." — THE CHRISTIAN SCIENCE MONITOR

"Adventurous and worthy." — SATURDAY REVIEW

"If you want to know what's on the cutting edge of American fiction, then these are the books you should be reading."
                    — UNITED PRESS INTERNATIONAL

On sale at bookstores everywhere, but if otherwise unavailable, may be ordered from us. You can use this coupon, or phone (800) 638-6460.

Please send me the Vintage Contemporaries books I have checked on the reverse. I am enclosing $ _____ (add $1.00 per copy to cover postage and handling). Send check or money order—no cash or CODs, please. Prices are subject to change without notice.

NAME _____

ADDRESS _____

CITY _____ STATE _____ ZIP _____

Send coupons to:
RANDOM HOUSE, INC., 400 Hahn Road, Westminster, MD 21157
ATTN: ORDER ENTRY DEPARTMENT
Allow at least 4 weeks for delivery.

VINTAGE
CONTEMPORARIES

___ Love Always by Ann Beattie	$5.95	74418-7
___ First Love and Other Sorrows by Harold Brodkey	$5.95	72970-6
___ The Debut by Anita Brookner	$5.95	72856-4
___ Cathedral by Raymond Carver	$4.95	71281-1
___ Bop by Maxine Chernoff	$5.95	75522-7
___ Dancing Bear by James Crumley	$5.95	72576-X
___ One to Count Cadence by James Crumley	$5.95	73559-5
___ The Wrong Case by James Crumley	$5.95	73558-7
___ The Last Election by Pete Davies	$6.95	74702-X
___ A Narrow Time by Michael Downing	$6.95	75568-5
___ Days Between Stations by Steve Erickson	$6.95	74685-6
___ Rubicon Beach by Steve Erickson	$6.95	75513-8
___ A Fan's Notes by Frederick Exley	$7.95	72915-3
___ A Piece of My Heart by Richard Ford	$5.95	72914-5
___ The Sportswriter by Richard Ford	$6.95	74325-3
___ The Ultimate Good Luck by Richard Ford	$5.95	75089-6
___ Fat City by Leonard Gardner	$5.95	74316-4
___ Within Normal Limits by Todd Grimson	$5.95	74617-1
___ Airships by Barry Hannah	$5.95	72913-7
___ Dancing in the Dark by Janet Hobhouse	$5.95	72588-3
___ November by Janet Hobhouse	$6.95	74665-1
___ Fiskadoro by Denis Johnson	$5.95	74367-9
___ The Stars at Noon by Denis Johnson	$5.95	75427-1
___ Asa, as I Knew Him by Susanna Kaysen	$4.95	74985-5
___ A Handbook for Visitors From Outer Space by Kathryn Kramer	$5.95	72989-7
___ The Chosen Place, the Timeless People by Paule Marshall	$6.95	72633-2
___ Suttree by Cormac McCarthy	$6.95	74145-5
___ The Bushwhacked Piano by Thomas McGuane	$5.95	72642-1
___ Nobody's Angel by Thomas McGuane	$6.95	74738-0
___ Something to Be Desired by Thomas McGuane	$4.95	73156-5
___ To Skin a Cat by Thomas McGuane	$5.95	75521-9
___ Bright Lights, Big City by Jay McInerney	$5.95	72641-3
___ Ransom by Jay McInerney	$5.95	74118-8
___ River Dogs by Robert Olmstead	$6.95	74684-8
___ Norwood by Charles Portis	$5.95	72931-5
___ Clea & Zeus Divorce by Emily Prager	$6.95	75591-X
___ A Visit From the Footbinder by Emily Prager	$6.95	75592-8
___ Mohawk by Richard Russo	$6.95	74409-8
___ Anywhere But Here by Mona Simpson	$6.95	75559-6
___ Carnival for the Gods by Gladys Swan	$6.95	74330-X
___ Myra Breckinridge and Myron by Gore Vidal	$8.95	75444-1
___ The Car Thief by Theodore Weesner	$6.95	74097-1
___ Taking Care by Joy Williams	$5.95	72912-9